My Own

Eni Aluko

Grosvenor House
Publishing Limited

This book is published by
Grosvenor House Publishing Ltd
Link House
140 The Broadway, Tolworth, Surrey, KT6 7HT.
www.grosvenorhousepublishing.co.uk

A CIP record for this book
is available from the British Library

ISBN 978-1-80381-602-9
eBook ISBN 978-1-80381-721-7

Disclaimer

This story is based on actual events. However, some of the
characters, names, businesses and organisations were changed
but the rest has been told exactly as it occurred.

Chapter One
Me before You

November 2013

"Morning, Tinuke."

I smiled at Jim, the office manager, as I breezed past him en route to my desk. No sooner had I removed my jacket, then he coughed. I knew what was coming, and to be honest, the joke was starting to wear a bit thin. Not that I'd ever found it funny to begin with.

He focused on me and said, "Why aren't you married yet?"

Everyone put on a laugh. He was their boss after all, and a bit of crawling now and then never did anyone any harm. I just smiled, shook my head and got on with my work.

What he, and for that matter all the English people in the office, didn't understand was this was never meant as a joke. I was one of the few Nigerians to work at the bank. They constantly asked me when I was going to get married, but they were deadly serious. Coming from Nigeria, the happiest day of my life was long overdue and my independence was frowned upon.

Five of my colleagues appeared from nowhere, all eager to have a chat and catch up with the weekend's news. About ten minutes' gossiping passed before we felt Jim's disapproving stare. In no time at all, the room was filled with the sound of clunking keys.

Jim had his faults, but he was a laugh. On Friday afternoon, he'd follow the Regional Manager out of his office, grinning from ear to ear. He then clapped his hands to gain everyone's attention and asked who was up for a team night out. I wasn't the first to raise my hand, but I wasn't the last either.

We were all sitting around talking at the bar when Jim sidled up to me and asked everyone to give us a minute. He often used these outings to have a quiet word with one of us in a more informal setting, so no one batted an eyelid. Trouble was, he'd been knocking them back all night, and by now he was inebriated, to say the least. He drained every last drop of lager from his glass, demanded a refill from the bartender and said I was up for promotion.

I let out a laugh to hide the confusion on my face. He told me he was being promoted and the Regional Manager wanted someone to take his place, and he'd put a word in for me. I nodded and said OK suspiciously.

I was about to ask for more details, when he leant back too far. I reached out to grab him, but I couldn't stop him toppling backwards. Moments later he was on the floor, rubbing his backside with one hand and removing the bar stool from his chest with the other. But the best was still to come. He dug his heels into the polished floor, pulled back his arms in a rowing motion and started humming 'Row, row, row your boat' in the puddle of lager he'd just created.

When I finally composed myself, I asked an onlooking guy to help him to his feet. As he did so, he suggested to

Jim that it might be time for him to go home. So Jim called for a taxi and went to wait outside, where no doubt he got up to more mischief.

The others appeared from the other side of the bar, all eager to find out what all the commotion was about. When they saw Jim's unoccupied stool, they looked at me inquisitively, until they saw the lager stain, when it all became clear. I explained what had happened, and we all laughed till it hurt.

A girl who I'd become good friends with took Jim's stool. When I relayed the story in full, she leant back and fought to keep her balance, just as Jim had. She, however, won the fight. At that moment, I thought about mentioning my promotion, but decided not to be hasty. Then she reached out, grabbed hold of my shoulder to steady herself and told me I was a laugh. I returned the compliment, and she thanked me from the bottom of her heart.

Not long after, someone put 'one way or Another' by One direction on the jukebox, and I forgot about Jim. Later on I decided it was the drink talking, so I dismissed it completely. And on that Monday morning, there was no mention of my upcoming promotion, so I decided to let things be, for fear of causing embarrassment to us both.

By mid morning, the Monday morning feeling had passed. It was approaching lunchtime when the girl sitting next to me realised that she'd been working in silence for far too long and announced that she was starving. Then followed a brief chat about what we all fancied for lunch, and even Jim threw in a contribution.

That's what it was like working in a bank in London. You worked hard and played hard all day long, until it was time to go home and you needed to let your hair down.

Like many City workers, my release was the gym. On Monday and Thursday nights I attended classes and got to know the other regulars. And on Tuesday, Wednesday and Friday we each did our own thing. We all got to know each other quite well. There were a couple of single women around my age, and they were happy being single. Being with them came as a relief, as they accepted me as I was, without putting pressure on me to get married.

We enjoyed each other's company, and afterwards we'd sit in the bar and enjoy a tipple before heading our separate ways. We all had each other's numbers, so it was easy to keep in touch. So, with the gym crew and my friends at work, I rarely had time to catch my breath. It seemed that everyone wanted a piece of me. I was in my element.

Along with my newfound financial independence, I became a bit materialistic. It was the first time in a while that I had money to spare at the end of the month, so I went through a phase of being a shopaholic. I'd often go up West after work or on a Saturday and return with a load of gear: handbags, jackets, blouses, all made by the most sought-after designer brands. Sometimes I'd meet up with friends for a coffee, laden with shopping bags.

It wasn't just the social life that I found so appealing. I loved the work side of my job. Going into the office each day, dressed in a smart skirt and white blouse, I felt like I could achieve anything I wanted to. I was financially independent, in my prime years and living life to the max. I had the world at my feet, and no one was going to get in my way.

I had my fair share of admirers at work. Whenever one of the guys from another department came in, they'd always say hi and ask how I was doing. Sometimes they got a bit playful, looking back over their shoulders and winking. All the guys laughed, and the girls told me to ignore their advances, in a jokey type of way.

Most guys at the bank were funny and enjoyed a laugh, all day long. But I wouldn't describe any of them as being a laugh, not in the way that Jim was.

As November drew to a close, people started mentioning Christmas, and the atmosphere became a bit more relaxed. When the decorations went up, talk started, not just of the main Christmas party, but of what we were going to do as a team. In the end we decided to go out for a meal, and once again Jim got absolutely blotto as he revelled in his role of court jester.

Waiting for the right moment, he pulled me to one side and mentioned the promotion again. I laughed it off and told him to go and sober up, but he was more insistent this time. Then he pulled out his phone and showed me a text from the Regional Manager. It was true. Jim was being promoted, and I was taking his place.

Jim didn't stipulate whether I should keep it to myself or not, so I decided to keep it quiet, just to be on the safe side. Besides, we were all having a great time.

The following Monday, it was the main Christmas party. I got to talk to people I wouldn't usually have spoken to. The food was delicious, but no one noticed, as the drink was even better. I found myself at the centre of a group of guys, all fighting like a flock of peacocks to get my attention. But I was having none of it. I just enjoyed their attention and played along with their banter. Then the Regional Manager's boss, who was right at the top of the bank's hierarchy, banged on his glass with a spoon. He got up to make his customary speech in which he thanked us all for our hard work and wished us a merry Christmas.

The party continued for an hour or so after that, until the bigwig said farewell. Just minutes later, the room was practically deserted, and the waitresses were rushing round picking up all the dirty crockery. They tutted at the state of the white tablecloths on the top table.

As I was leaving, the Regional Manager, who hadn't seemed quite as important among the company he'd been keeping, pulled me aside and congratulated me on my promotion.

A couple of weeks into the new year it was customary for everyone to go to a huge conference where people were put in the spotlight and named and shamed. When all the jokey awards had been finished, such as biggest poser, worst haircut, etc., it was time to get down to business. Then it got right to the end, the climax of the evening, the award that actually meant something. Yes, it was time to announce the employee of the year.

I spoke to the girl behind me occasionally, so I whispered something to her over my shoulder, and we shared a laugh. I was still trying to stifle my laughter when they called my name out. I focused on the stage, just to make sure I hadn't imagined it. Then I got up and walked through the clapping and back-slapping towards the stage. The bigwig who had been at the party shook my hand and gave me the award. Once all the clapping and cheering had subsided, he announced my promotion, which I think was meant to be a surprise.

Later on Jim took us out to celebrate, but for some reason it wasn't quite the same. I noticed one or two people sneering at me from a distance and blanking me when I tried to make conversation. Most people were friendly, but as I said, it wasn't quite the same.

I spent the weekend basking in my glory. I tried to phone some of the girls from work, but they were always busy. However, the gym lot were delighted for me, so we had a glass of wine and, the ultimate indulgence for a gym-goer, a Big Mac and fries. Boy, did they taste good.

The men I knew at work soon made me the butt of their jokes. It was all the sexist stuff: sleeping with the boss, blow jobs in the cupboard, that kind of thing. I put a brave face on at first and even managed to force out a laugh, but then I noticed a sinister undertone to their voices. I studied their faces and concluded that each one of them thought they deserved the promotion more than me.

One Saturday, a couple of weeks before I was due to take over from Jim, I woke up in high spirits. The sun was shining, so I felt like making the most of it. I knew none of the girls from work would be interested in going out, so I went to the gym to see who was there. I did meet someone I knew, but she had to go straight home. So, after a quick mineral water, we went our separate ways. I was going to Oxford Street for some serious retail therapy.

It was a great afternoon, as good as it gets when you're out shopping on your own. I found this amazing bag and outfit, then at about five, I walked to Tottenham

Court Road tube station. I was in such high spirits that I decided to visit my friend instead of going home.

"I've had a great day," I said, taking my new stuff out of the bags to show her. "Here, have a look at these."

But my friend shook her head and turned away. "Tinuke, don't you think it's time you got married?"

"What? Oh... I thought you were on my side."

"I *am* on your side, Tinuke, but I mean... look at you."

I played dumb. "What?"

Oh, don't play the fool with me. You're 29, you have no husband and no kids. Just what do you have to show for your life?"

Maybe she was right. "I just want to enjoy myself for a while. Look, I really enjoy working at the bank, and lots of women there are single."

"Lots of *English* women. Are you English? No, you're Nigerian, and don't forget it."

I picked up my bags. "I won't. I haven't. I'm going now. Goodbye."

"Goodbye, Tinuke."

The next week or so after that encounter wasn't easy. The Nigerian community had been saying that to me for a while, but I had managed to push it to the back of my mind. It's not that I had abandoned my Nigerian roots, it's just that a large part of me was English too. It was definitely a tough one, which weighed so heavily on me that people at work started to notice a change in my demeanour. When my friends from the gym phoned to ask why they hadn't seen me, I didn't feel like answering.

Then I started to perk up. I called my friend to patch things up, and she invited me round to her house the next day. This put something resembling a smile back on my face, if only temporarily.

As soon as I opened the door and saw her smiling, I knew things were all right between us. She led me inside and through to the living room, where we used to sit and have a natter. Then, as I looked into the room over her shoulder, I saw a guy sitting on an armchair that was usually unoccupied when I came to visit.

"Tinuke, this is Femi."

I didn't know what to think. Why would she go inviting strange men—*Oh, I get it.* I wanted to throttle her.

"Femi, this is Tinuke, my friend I was telling you about." It was obvious they'd been plotting this for some time.

Femi stood up and offered me his hand. I placed my hand over his without making any attempt at all to grip. His hands were big, completely enveloping mine, and they were noticeably soft.

I looked over my shoulder at my friend, who was standing there grinning, completely oblivious to the feeling of awkwardness her meddling had created. "I'll leave you to it then," she said, leaving the room. I faced the door for as long as I could without making it obvious that I didn't want to make eye contact.

He was the first to speak up. He told me I was wearing a nice dress, which I wasn't, but I gave him a polite smile anyway. I could tell right away that he was a quiet guy who liked to keep his cards close to his chest.

"Your friend is quite a character, isn't she?"

This time I couldn't duck the question. "Suppose so." Immediately after I said it, the wall of awkwardness came tumbling down, so we engaged in a short conversation in which he tolerated me. He was a Master's student, and I said I worked in a bank.

I continued the conversation, just because it was better than sitting in silence staring through the window. But I soon started to feel more and more at ease. After about half an hour or so, we even shared a bit of a laugh. He was hard work though. My first impressions were correct. He was reluctant to tell me anything about himself, so much so that I almost gave up trying. He repositioned himself on the couch and his hand brushed mine. Yes, they were just as soft as I remembered.

Eventually, he asked me out on a date. His friend was throwing a party somewhere and he thought I'd enjoy it. I gave it some thought and decided that since I had nothing else to do that night I'd give it a go.

I could have killed him there and then for the way he announced it to my friend when she made her return. She beamed at me, offered us her congratulations and showed him to the door. On her return she was looking as smug as I'd ever seen her. It was going to be a long time before I could forgive her for inflicting this on me.

One positive was that when Jim made his customary Monday morning dig at me, it was like water off a duck's back. I just switched on my computer and started my day, unaffected. At that moment I felt grateful to my friend, but it soon passed.

I knew if I made an effort and it didn't work out, my friend, while meaning well, would be absolutely infuriating. So I made no effort at all. I paid more attention to my appearance for a Monday morning shopping trip.

Femi looked just as scruffy as me. He'd been quite well dressed when I had seen him before: smart designer jeans, designer t-shirt and loafers. The fact that his jeans were all baggy and his t-shirt looked like it had been screwed up and pulled straight from the tumble dryer, told me that he had the same attitude as me towards our date. To begin with I felt put out by this, but when we got chatting, it became an ice-breaker that paved the way for a thoroughly enjoyable evening.

He acted like a gentleman on the way to the party, starting from the moment we met. He led me down the stairs to his car. And then he held open the passenger door for me to get in. He had a nice car. Not new, a few years old, but it was well kept. If this was anything to go by, he liked to keep up appearances through effort rather than throwing his cash around. This impressed me to no end.

As we drove to the party, I couldn't help throwing the occasional glance at him, just to see if he was doing the same thing. The scruffy attire that he'd put on in a hurry, for the first time made me feel a bit hurt.

Roughly halfway there he stopped at a set of lights. He turned to speak to me, and we shared a bit of a laugh. So when the lights changed, he was distracted. A couple of girls, obviously on a night out, stepped out onto the road. He slammed the heel of his hand into the centre of the steering wheel and sounded his horn, just a few seconds too long. The girls, startled, turned round to wave an apology. I was fully expecting him to wave back and gesture as if it was no problem, but he didn't. Instead he wound down the window and hurled abuse at them. Again, in my opinion, he went a bit too far.

He was quiet for the remainder of the journey. Once we left the main road, we went through a labyrinth of side roads, turning this way and that, until we arrived. It wasn't the kind of place I'd have felt comfortable in walking on my own. His presence made me feel safe and protected, so I had no problem at all leaving the safety of the car. I was expecting to have a thoroughly enjoyable evening.

A group of men about the same age as Femi were arguing by the door. I got the impression that, while they were clearly very passionate, it was all very friendly. A fit of laughter broke out as we walked towards them.

Femi put his hand to his mouth and coughed to grab their attention. They each slapped his back as they welcomed him into the huddle. Within seconds the atmosphere grew a lot more hostile. I took the opportunity to observe them closely, Femi in particular. He was definitely the most belligerent of them, arguing for argument's sake.

He was still angry as he led me inside. His expression, and the way he kept looking over his shoulder to glower at the men that were supposed to be his friends, told me that.

The pattern continued all night long. People would be debating an issue in a totally amicable manner, and he would join in and within minutes they'd be shouting angrily. But no one's perfect though. There have been plenty of thoroughly decent people throughout history who have been like this, and in many cases, people liked them for it. All he was doing was cranking things up a notch, and there was nothing wrong with that.

I didn't know anyone, but that didn't make me a wallflower. I soon made friends, got talking with the women and shared a few laughs. As the night drew near, people started to get increasingly inebriated and I started to worry that Femi would be in no fit state to drive me home. By the time the host declared the party to be over, I was certain of it.

So I said goodbye on Femi's behalf, smiled and called for a taxi.

I didn't hear from him for a day or so after that. He was in a bad way when I left him, so I assumed he needed time to recover from his hangover. This gave me some breathing space, which I used to reflect. He'd been a total gentleman before the party, before the drink and his friends started to have an influence. His friends. Yes, that must have been it. I decided that his friends were obviously a bad influence on him and he needed a good woman to make him see the error of his ways. By the time he called, I was starting to convince myself that I was up for the task.

When he asked me for another date, I said yes. This time I said yes because I wanted to.

So our romance gathered pace. Once he came out of his shell, he was fun to be around, and the sex was great too. When I started feeling gratitude towards my friend for introducing us, I surprised even myself. It was all a bit of a whirlwind and there was no time at all to stop and think it through. About a month after we first met, things started to get a bit more serious.

Chapter Two
Pregnancy: Bubbles Burst

From that moment on, his attitude grew colder by the day. Not only that, but I had to put my life on hold, so I felt alone. More alone than I had for a long time. This gave me time to think. I concluded that our relationship was on the rocks, and if I didn't act, it could soon be damaged beyond repair.

So I confided in my friend. According to her, this is how men react when they first find out that a woman is pregnant. They always get moody and spend time in isolation. I had to put up with it and wait for him to come round, whenever that might be. I didn't like what I was hearing, so I tried remonstrating with her, saying that it wasn't fair and that I needed his support more than ever. But she wouldn't listen. She dug her heels in and said that I had become too English. A Nigerian woman wouldn't have my attitude.

In week sixteen I found a letter on the doormat. I picked it up, held it between my thumb and forefinger, then turned it over. It was from the bank. I'd still been emailing Wendy since I last saw her, so I assumed it was from her. I had no reason to suspect it was bad news at all.

They were going to terminate my contract, which was corporate speak for "You're sacked". Of course, they didn't give a reason, but I knew what it was about. It was because I was having so much time off sick, and then there was going to be maternity leave. I took the letter back to the couch and sat down to contemplate. They'd stabbed me in the back, but worse than that, it left us in a quandary financially. As Femi was unemployed, there was going to be a rocky road ahead.

I'd never been sacked from anything in my life, so first there was the stigma, the blot on my CV that was going to make it virtually impossible to get another job. Then there were the financial implications. I wasn't going to get any maternity pay, and then after I would have had the baby, I'd be an unemployed mother, with a useless father. I switched on the computer to do some quick research about state benefits for unemployed mothers.

This was the last thing I needed on top of my hyperemesis. My only hope was that Femi would finally grow up and take his share of the responsibility.

I was at my lowest ebb at that time. I spent the next couple of days in a daze, not really noticing when the days ended and when the nights began. Then I woke up one morning feeling well enough to go into the office and confront Wendy.

I could hardly recognise her when I first saw her. Although I was still seething, I managed to be polite. I smiled and said hi, but there wasn't a flicker of emotion on her face. She just sighed and asked me what I was doing there. So I asked, quite calmly, if I could go to her office for a quick word. She sighed and said OK, as long as I made it quick.

Things didn't go to plan. I'd only just touched the letter in my pocket when I got the urge to throw up. I excused myself and ran to the ladies, where I vomited over and over, until there was nothing left to come up. On the way out I passed the cleaner, whom I knew well, and told her I had made a mess. 'Not to worry,' she said and went inside to clean up.

My boss was standing at the door to her office, smiling at me for the first time that morning. This time she patted me on the back and told me to follow her back into her office.

Once inside, she told me to shut the door and then walked towards me, smiling and with her arms open. Then she hugged me, and we both got a bit emotional. I felt bad about mentioning the letter, but I still did it. To my surprise, she shook her head and said it was a mistake. She added that my job would still be open when I was ready and to stay in touch.

That was the last bit of good news I have had for a while.

By this time my hyperemesis was really bad. I spent most of the day either in bed or laid up on the couch, as I just wasn't well enough to do anything else. I had to keep a bottle next to me at all times, because I was salivating all day long. I vomited up to twenty times a day, and each time it left me feeling like I'd just been booted in the stomach. Sometimes I was able to go to the toilet, but most of the time I just had to lean over and puke into a bowl. Inevitably, sometimes I missed, and there was the odd spillage. I wanted to get up and clean up a bit, make the air smell a bit fresher, but I just couldn't manage it. The place stank to high heaven of vomit, which, in turn, made me vomit even more.

And just when I thought things couldn't get any worse, I realised he was trying to control me.

I was using my current account for everyday living expenses, but that started to run dry, so, with little choice, I gave him access to my savings. I only did this because I was unable to go out and get food for myself, so I was reliant on him. I told him what I wanted and had an idea in my head of how much it would cost. But when he came back, almost everything he bought was more than I had expected to pay. I told myself that he had my best interests at heart, and let him continue to do this without protest. Deep down, I knew that I should say something, but I wasn't feeling up to the inevitable arguing that would follow.

I've always been prudent with money, even before I worked in a bank. I grew up with the attitude that if you can save money by shopping around or using your own resourcefulness, you should do so. Femi didn't see things this way. He believed that if something was twice the price, it was better. He also felt he was too good to be seen in a cheaper shop or buying brands that were not so well known.

Other people's money is more precious than your own. This is another thing I've been brought up to believe. When I was living with my parents, I'd be reluctant to put the central heating on when they were not at home. If they were buying something for me, I'd never choose the most expensive item. This is how I assumed most people to be. But Femi was different. He was more than happy to spend my cash and be less generous with his own.

In this way, we were worlds apart, but I knew if I stuck to my guns, he'd go on and on, for days sometimes. So I decided it would be less trouble to do as he wanted. It was worth paying the extra money to keep him in a good mood.

When he was wasteful with my money, I could feel myself boiling over inside, but I had to swallow my anger. He was making me act like someone I wasn't.

There was something else. I found out that he was up to his eyeballs in debt, probably through gambling, but I never got down to the particulars. Each time I looked at my statement and noticed my dwindling savings, I saw that he had taken some of my money. I couldn't let this go, so I approached him about it. The bickering went on all day, until I just wished I had kept my mouth shut. According to him, he did have money, but the bank had closed down his account. I knew this was a lie.

Keeping it all in was starting to wear me down. I was reluctant to talk to him about anything, and when I did speak up, I had to yield to his opinion for my own mental wellbeing. But on this occasion I decided to take the plunge and confront him about it. I knew he'd argue incessantly, until it was just arguing for argument's sake, but I suspected that this time he'd get angry and I'd end up wishing I had kept my mouth shut more than ever.

I was right; he was angry. He didn't scream and shout though. He shook his head, smiled and muttered, "I don't believe this." Then he said that I was making things up and that he hadn't spent a single penny without my permission.

Thankfully, though, he was rarely in the house. Given different circumstances, I might have gotten suspicious sooner, but I was just too sick to bother myself with it. Then one night, when he came in at around eight, he disappeared into our bedroom and left me alone to do the dishes after dinner. I turned the tap off and enjoyed a rare moment of silence. I heard a strange moaning sound that could only have been one thing. He was obviously watching porn. After I had finished washing up, I attempted to check on him, but I got sick. By the time I came out of the bathroom, he was putting his coat on. He said he was just going to the shops to buy something he forgot on his way in.

So then I started being extra vigilant. I'd keep an ear out whenever he was in a different room, trying to ascertain what he was up to. Then on one occasion I heard something I wished I hadn't. He was on the phone, and from the way he was talking, it definitely wasn't to one of his friends.

On top of everything else, he was cheating on me. I didn't know what to do. I had to confide in someone or else I was going to go insane.

It came as a great relief when my friend showed up. Femi had gone out to the shops for something he'd forgotten a couple of hours earlier, giving my friend and I a moment to ourselves. I relayed to her my frustrations, adding that I was close to breaking point. She smiled and told me it would be OK in the end. Up until then, I thought she was on my side.

When Femi showed up, she made a right fuss of him, saying he must be looking forward to being a father and all. Femi smiled and managed to convince her that it was going to be the most significant moment of his life. She just looked at me and shook her head, insinuating that I had been imagining things when I'd confided in her a moment earlier. Then he left the room for a while for some reason that I didn't quite catch. I took the opportunity to further elaborate to my friend, hoping that once I explained properly, she'd understand. She listened, faked some sympathy, and then asked me if I was sure I hadn't made a mistake. I insisted over and over that I hadn't, so in the end she said she was going to confront him. I begged her not to, but she was certain that the misunderstanding had to be cleared up once and for all. He reappeared before I had a chance to protest.

"Femi," she said, as he sat on the armchair.

He smiled at her, going completely over the top in his attempt to appear amicable. "Yes."

"I believe you've been spending Tinuke's money."

I looked straight ahead.

He glared at the floor. Seconds later his head rose inch by inch until our eyes locked. "Oh, not this again. Come on, I thought we had cleared this up?"

"No, we—"

"We did, and we decided that you were wrong. Remember?"

"No!" I turned to my friend. "No, we didn't decide this. We did nothing of the sort."

Femi jumped in before she could reply. "We did agree on this, honey." He turned to my friend. "She's been doing this all the time lately." He lowered his voice to a whisper. "I think she's going a bit..." He tapped on his temple.

Then they both turned as one and gave me the kind of condescending smile that I had only ever seen on the faces of politicians previously.

"Tinuke," my friend said, reaching over to pat my knee. "Tinuke, you have to get over this."

I couldn't take it any more. "He's been wasting my money. I'm not making anything up."

Femi just shook his head, shrugged and said, "See what I mean?"

Then my friend stood up and declared it was time she got home to start on her husband's dinner. As she was about to close the door behind her, she looked over her shoulder and said, "We'll get you some help, Tinuke. Don't worry."

Then as soon as she had gone, Femi leaned over and said, "See, everyone thinks you're crazy. It isn't just me, dear, is it?"

By this time, I had lost the will to go on arguing, so I just stood up and staggered into the kitchen to get a bite to eat.

He continued to appear with all sorts of expensive, unnecessary items. And each time I confronted him, he said I was going crazy. Sometimes he'd ask me if he should call my friend, as if I was mentally unstable. I've never felt so infuriated or trapped in my life.

Things soon went from bad to worse. I stopped accusing him of wasting money, because he just kept on calling me crazy. On one occasion he carried out his threat and invited my friend over, who told me if I didn't stop, she'd have to get me to a doctor. I thought that if my friend had turned on me in that way, then maybe I was losing my mind. Perhaps I should make an appointment with a doctor. Then he started saying that all my close people had turned their backs on me, and if I carried on like this, I'd be ostracised by the entire

Nigerian community. Then I'd be alone, wondering why it was that people didn't like me.

The psychological abuse continued. Any time I said anything he didn't like, he just threatened to call my friend or, worse still, ask my doctor if he could have me sectioned. I wanted to scream out. To go on the rampage. To smash up the flat and throw something so hard it would knock his head off. But I knew this would be playing right into his hands, so instead I just sat there quietly, timid, beaten, too scared to talk to anyone.

Things got progressively worse throughout the pregnancy. He regularly called me stupid or said that I was wrong about something that I knew much more than him about. Whenever I talked about something of interest to me, he'd just sigh and talk about himself.

There was absolutely no reasoning with him. Sure, all couples have arguments from time to time, but he never met me halfway. He refused to see anything from my point of view, so it was always me who ended up apologising and giving in. It was the same with any subject. It could be something on the news that we disagreed about, one of my friends or even something as trivial as the perfume I was wearing. He just couldn't, or refused, to see anyone's point of view other than his own.

I've always had a reputation for being a well-dressed, fashionable type of person who keeps up to date with all the latest trends. I soon became too large for this, so I had to settle for frumpy maternity clothes. He was quick to jump on this, as if he had been waiting for a moment of weakness. It felt like he was a predator watching my every move.

Sometimes, as I sat there on my own, getting bigger and bigger, my days at the bank felt increasingly distant. I'd try to talk about it, asking him if he thought I could resume my career and pick up where I had left off. Thinking about this raised my spirits immeasurably. All I wanted was his encouragement, but instead he told me I wasn't as successful as I imagined. He even said it was another example of how I remembered things wrongly.

On one occasion he came in and walked straight past me into the bedroom. As this wasn't an unusual occurrence, I pretended not to notice. Then I could hear him moving things around, accompanied by the occasional bang and bout of cursing. I thought that whatever he was doing, it sounded like he needed some help. I found him with his back to me, rooting through the cupboard that he used to keep his personal stuff in. I held my breath. Completely oblivious to my presence, he pulled out what looked like a laptop bag. He turned around.

"Oh, I'm sorry, I was just—"

"Touch this and I'll kill you. I'm not messing around. I'll kill you."

I knew he was serious, but that didn't stop me from being curious.

Until then, I thought alone meant living in solitude physically, with no one to talk to or help you through difficult times. Although many people do experience this type of loneliness, lots of people feel lonely inside. It is quite possible to be alone and have your friends and family around if no one is listening to you. And people you thought were on your side were siding with your enemy. When this happens, it feels like you've been stabbed in the back, creating a wound that goes so deep that you feel wholly incapacitated. This was the situation I now found myself in. It would have been hard for anyone to cope with, but a pregnant woman? A new mother with no prior experience? With all the hormones and emotional turmoil floating around anyway, it is a wonder that I didn't go off the rails completely. The fact that I didn't is something I'll always be proud of.

Chapter Three
Mr Not-so-charming

"Anything else?"

"Err, yeah, I'll have some orange juice please."

"No problem."

I smiled to myself. He was doing his best to take care of me now. Maybe he just needed some time to adjust. "Wait a minute."

He looked at me over his shoulder." "Yes?"

"Get something for yourself. Get a CD or something."

He smiled, said thank you and left me to sit on the couch alone. There are many drawbacks to letting someone else use your bank account. You have to be able to trust them like they're your own family, or you'll spend all your time worrying what they're up to. I decided I was going to try to trust him from now on. Maybe it had all been in my mind after all. There was a plus side too: if I wanted to say thank you or just give him a gift because I felt like it, I could. This gave me a warm feeling inside that put me in a happy mood. I decided that when he came back, we'd put his CD on while I made something to eat. Everything was going to be great.

"Hi, Tinuke, I've got your stuff. Here's your orange juice."

"Thanks." I made my way over to the kitchen to pour some juice into a glass and put the food away. There was no CD. "Didn't you get a CD?"

"Oh yeah, but not a CD."

I smiled. "What did you get then?"

He pulled out a box set of five movies he liked. I couldn't help but take a quick peek at the receipt. He had spent £70 on them. "Great. Should we put one on after we've eaten?"

"Oh, we could."

So I began making dinner as planned. I was looking forward to an enjoyable evening, with a nice meal followed by a film, even though we had differing tastes. Dinner was a struggle for me to cook, given my sickness and all, but it was worth it in the end. Afterwards I glanced at the pile of dishes and asked if he could help me, since I had spent a few hours cooking. I thought it was a given that he'd say yes. Who wouldn't? He sighed and said OK, but he'd do them in his own time.

Half an hour later the dishes were still on the draining rack, and there was no sign of him. I knew I wouldn't be able to relax knowing they were there, so I did them myself. I felt indignant to begin with, but it didn't take me long to do, so no harm done.

He'd come over to England to study and had to leave without his certificate. Unlike me, he had no family over here and no one to support him. I was all he had. I spent a moment reflecting over the previous few weeks and concluded that I was to blame for at least half of the arguments. Things would be better between us if I could find a way of helping him. I decided that, like anyone, he would be far happier if he had a job.

I found him sitting on the couch watching one of the DVDs with his earphones in. "Femi?" No response. "Femi, can I have a word please?" I tapped him on the shoulder.

He took his earphones out. "For God's sake, can't you see I'm busy?"

"Yes. I just wanted a chat about something. I thought I might be able to help you out."

"Fine. Let me finish this and then I'm all yours."

I sat at the other end of the couch watching TV for about an hour, until he pulled his earphones out and switched off his laptop.

"Femi?" He made eye contact for a fraction of a second and then started playing with his phone. By this time, I wanted to snatch the phone from his hands and throw it on the floor. "Femi?"

He dropped his phone onto the couch. "What do you want?"

"I just want to talk. Listen, I've noticed that you've been a bit down lately and—"

He sighed.

"And I want to try to help."

"How can *you* help *me*?"

"I thought—How much do you owe the university again?" I asked this, even though I knew full well it was £700.

"Seven hundred pounds. Why?"

"Well, I thought—I'd like to pay for it."

His face lit up. "Oh, thanks, babe."

I'd done it. He looked happier than he had for some time. "Well, I thought it might help you get a job. Save you moping around here all day and—"

He sighed. "Because it might help me get a job? You can't do anything without thinking of yourself, can you?"

I wanted to strangle him, or worse. "No, it's not that. I think you misunderstood me, I just—"

"OK, you can pay my fees."

"Fine. I'll do it tomorrow."

I was hurt and angry. Now he'd thrown the gesture back in my face. This was the last thing I'd wanted to do. But I had said it now, so if I backed out, I'd have to spell it out to him over and over that he wasn't being fair. And even then, *I'd* be the one having to apologise.

It was on the Monday when we had the discussion about his fees; by Thursday it was something else.

He stormed in, slammed the door and threw my bank card in my face.

"What's this?" I said, completely nonplussed.

"I saw your balance on the cash machine. Why didn't you tell me you had money?"

He'd found me out. I was in no place to judge him for the mysterious laptop bag. "Because it's my money, Femi."

"You didn't answer my question. Why didn't you tell me?"

"I-I just didn't think it was important."

"But we could have done a lot with this money. You've been lying to me."

"It's spoken for though."

"What do you mean?"

"I mean it's for a specific purpose. It hasn't got anything to do with you." I braced myself for the backlash. To my surprise, he just shrugged and said fine.

I could tell it wasn't fine though, because he was moody for the rest of the night. Now he knew, he would to take his spending to a whole new level. I cursed myself for being so lax. Why hadn't I had the foresight to open a new account and transfer most of the money into it?

A week or so later, I got my bank statement. I noticed the anomaly straight away. I had been letting him use my card to buy food, which showed a great deal of trust on my part. In a funny way, I thought this gesture might have brought us closer together, because it would demonstrate to me that he could be trusted and I'd see a different side to him. At least that's what I had been hoping for.

It was more with a sense of disappointment than anger that I noticed he had been syphoning money from my account. He had been using my cash mainly to pay off some debts, but he'd also sent money to some of his family in Nigeria. I should have known better. He'd made a mockery of me, just like he had when I'd offered to buy him a CD by way of thanks for taking care of me. I had given him far too much credit. Lesson learnt. However, I wasn't going to just leave it at that. Not this time. The minute he resurfaced, I was going to confront him, and to hell with the consequences.

He always knew how to wriggle out of things. As soon as he came in, I could see he was in a good mood. He was smiling, talking excitedly about a job he had seen advertised, and had been to the shops to get me some orange juice. How could I confront him now?

He was in such high spirits that I started to feel a bit anxious as we ate. I really didn't want to spoil things, but I couldn't let him get away with this, and I knew that if

I didn't do it right away, I'd go on putting it off until I'd learnt to live with it.

So after we finished eating, I waited until we were settled on the couch and I confronted him. "Femi?"

He smiled at me and patted my thigh, which he hadn't done for quite some time. "Yes?"

My mouth went dry. "I got a bank statement this morning."

"Oh, OK." He laughed and shook his head like he was wondering what this had to do with him.

"I noticed an anomaly."

"What kind of anomaly?" Cool as a cucumber. "The kind where—I don't have as much money as I thought. And… it looks to me like you've been taking it."

He stared at the wall in front of him without flinching. "I see. What makes you think that?"

"Because it looks like you've been using some to pay off your debts, and some to send to your family in Nigeria." I had to finish what I was saying before giving him a chance to reply, otherwise he'd never listen. "Do you have any outstanding debts you've been hiding from me?"

He turned to look at me for the first time. "Give me that." He held out his hand for me to pass him the bank statement. I couldn't wait to see how he was going to get out of this one.

"OK, I *have* been taking your money."

What? Was he owning up without making any kind of denial?

"Why?"

"Because I didn't think you'd mind. I'm up to my neck in debt and you have all this money lying around.

You offered to pay my uni debt, so I assumed you would have given me—"

"No, Femi, I hadn't given you permission for anything."

He sniggered. "Well, first you offer to help me and then you change your mind. What the—" He crashed his fist onto the coffee table. "I just can't stand living with you any more."

This was more like it. I had caught him red-handed, so he had to get creative to worm his way out. He was so convincing that I was starting to fall for it and question my own double standards. I had to try to buy some time. "How much in debt are you, Femi?"

"Oh, I don't know exactly. A lot, OK?"

"To who?"

"*I don't know*, just this and that. And the bank is accusing me of being a fraud."

Working in a bank as I did, I knew this was a lie. "So you don't know who you owe money to?"

"Oh, of course I do. I'm not some kind of imbecile."

The term man-child came to mind. "Who then?"

"Oh, I owe some rent arrears."

"How much?"

"I don't know exactly, about six months."

He owed six months' rent, and yet he was willing to go out and waste money like there was no tomorrow. He was just like an adolescent in the respect that he had yet to learn the value of money.

My sickness took a turn for the worse. Looking back, I think it was because of all the stress he was putting me under. Of course, doctors are not going to say that, because it's not really their place to throw around theories without any concrete proof, but it just seemed like too much of a coincidence. I was devoting so much of my energy to staying calm and avoiding arguments that I had nothing left to fight the hyperemesis.

It was all to no avail though. Femi could be like a dog with a bone at times. Now he had found out about my money, he was determined to get his claws on it. I'm not sure if he really did see it as his entitlement or if he was just opportunistic, but as always, he was persuasive. On more than one occasion I had to stop myself giving in to him when he asked for money to, supposedly, pay off his debts. I wanted to help, but experience told me that if I did, he'd go on taking my generosity for granted until it became the norm. And then it would be something else. I tried my very best not to judge and to tell myself he was in a difficult situation, but it was difficult with all the evidence that was stacking up against him. Some people just can't be helped.

I was feeling terrible, getting increasingly lethargic, and always tired. I just couldn't cope with the constant bickering. He found faults with me all the time, asked why I hadn't done this or that. It was clear as daylight that the underlying factor behind it all was my money. Part of me wanted to give in to him, let him spend it as he pleased, just for an easy life. But I wouldn't have been able to live with myself if I did this, so I decided I had to be strong. I had to find a way of getting rid of the money. Oh yes, it would be bad to begin with, but at least there would be no long-term ramifications that could affect my perception of myself.

I tried to think of ways to empty my account that wouldn't leave me short in years to come. I browsed the newspapers and visited various websites, trying to find an investment opportunity that wasn't too risky. They say that just getting a problem out in the open helps you think of a solution yourself, so I gave my mum a ring.

There was a house on the market in Nigeria. It was a nice house in a respectable area, but it had become a bit dilapidated over time. My mum thought I could make a lot of money by buying it cheap, doing some renovations and selling it on. I thought this was a great idea, but coming from a banking background, I knew the perils of making a snap decision. So I thanked my mum, told her I felt a whole lot better now and said I'd go away and think about it for a few days. If I decided to go ahead, it would cost me £16,000 to buy.

The first thing on my list, before I could even think about investing in the house, was to make some enquiries about the cost of renovations.

After spending so much time on the couch, too ill to move, this gave me something constructive to do. It cheered me up so much that the hyperemesis seemed to improve. In the end I found a company in Nigeria that looked like they could be trusted. My mum was right, it was a good investment. So I told her I would go ahead and send over £16,000 to buy the house.

He wasn't happy when he found out, but that had never been my concern. He could rant and rave and bicker as much as he wanted, but he'd never change the fact that I had managed to safeguard the money from my own fallibility. It felt like a huge victory. The trouble was, that's how Femi saw it too.

He was clever about it this time. It's like he had observed what buttons to press and learnt from it.

He didn't stop at picking faults all the time or laughing when something I was doing didn't work out; this time he took my friends aside whenever they came round and told them that my sickness was all in my head. As if that wasn't bad enough, he also insisted they forget about me. He could be a really charming and persuasive guy when he wanted to be, so I wasn't angry with my friends for believing him. I had been deceived many times myself.

By this time, the hyperemesis was unbearable. I was running to the bathroom about forty times a day. I was tempted many times to insist he take a look and then tell me if I really was imagining it, but that wouldn't have achieved a thing. He'd have come up with some way of worming his way out of it, just like he'd done when I'd asked him why was been taking money from my account. So I continued putting up with this, cursing myself for being so weak, until I struggled to look him in the eye. However, he had yet to reach the bottom of the pit.

Once, while he was out, I took out my phone and looked on Instagram to see what people were up to. Some people hate social media, but it kept me in the land of the living. I scrolled down a couple of screens, and then I saw it.

Femi had posted a picture of me looking my absolute worst. I stared at it for a moment, unable to breathe, asking myself how anyone could be so cruel. Then I noticed the caption. *Is this a good-looking woman?*

The door creaked open. I placed his phone back on the table and prayed that he wouldn't notice it had been moved. To my relief, he came over, dumped some orange juice on the table, then picked up his phone. Seconds later, I was on my own again. I tried not to dwell on the

Instagram picture, but I couldn't help it. I kept on torturing myself until I felt the urge to scream.

I really could have done with some support. My friends, though, were not all on my side, and besides, they had lives of their own to live. They had their own problems and difficulties, so the last thing they needed was me adding to their burden. So instead I had to sit there, day in, day out, suffering in silence, dreading the sound of his footsteps on the street outside. I started to think more and more about the contents of the mysterious black laptop bag. There might be some useful information in there, something that would explain his behaviour.

So, eventually, I decided to take a look, just to satisfy my curiosity. With my heart pounding in my throat, I opened the cupboard where I had seen it last and started searching. The more I searched, the more determined I became to discover what he was hiding. The door opened, and he burst in.

I slammed the closet door shut, which I instantly regretted. Then, to my relief, his phone rang, and he lingered in the kitchen. I took the opportunity to tiptoe back onto the couch, leaving it to chance that I hadn't left any evidence behind me.

When he came in, he studied me for a minute—like he knew exactly what I had been doing—before saying hello and walking into the bedroom. The closet door opened; I screwed my eyes and waited for his wrath.

He emerged from the bedroom smiling and asked how I felt. I spent the rest of the night, indeed the entire week, wondering how much he knew.

Chapter Four
Pregnancy Glow is such a Myth

I wiped the sickness from around my mouth and began the long, slow walk back to the couch. It was starting to smell. I closed my eyes, and an incredible feeling of relaxation took hold of me. But it didn't last long.

My head began to spin, and a ball of something wholly disgusting began its journey from the pit of my stomach to my mouth. I shifted my back up till my head was resting on the wall. Then, once I knew for sure, I made a dash to the bathroom, this time coming up short. I stared down at the mess for a second and immediately had to look away. I put my hands over my mouth, but it was all in vain.

I felt bad about leaving it there, in front of the bathroom door, but there was no choice. If I bent down to clean it up, I would only make the mess ten times worse. So, after wiping my mouth with a damp piece of kitchen roll, I staggered back to the couch and tried to relax. I managed to shut my eyes for about half an hour before the cycle started again.

I usually made it to the bathroom though, thankfully. I kept a bowl next to me for convenience, but sometimes it took me too long to position myself. I did have interludes where I was able to get up and do some cleaning, but I had to prioritise the stains by the bathroom, as there'd been no bowl to capture the majority of it. I could barely move, barely breathe without wanting to vomit, and my whole vicinity was stinking to high heaven. And to make matters worse, I had to rely on Femi to clean up after me.

Around October time I reached the point where I'd had enough. I had to battle to stop myself from vomiting in the taxi on my way to the hospital. I tried to walk unaided through the rotating doors into the reception, but the driver had to get out and help me, until a nurse saw me and took over.

I can't stand the smell of hospitals, never have been able to. It's a good thing that the nurse helped me to the waiting area, because if he hadn't, I'd have turned right back and gone home. Each time I turned a corner and saw more sick people, my headache got worse, which in turn made me want to vomit. The nurse did stop a few times and ask if I was OK, which gave me the strength to continue for a few more steps.

As soon as I sat down on one of those red, plastic chairs they have in all hospital waiting rooms, I leant forward and retched. I didn't vomit, but I wanted to. Thankfully, one of the nurses saw that I was in a bad way and fetched a trolley-bed for me to lie on. The hard bed with a half-inch mattress made me feel a hundred times better.

Being higher up than everyone else gave me a good view of the waiting area and the whole department. I saw a woman in a white gown being helped out of a side room by a doctor. From the look on her face, she was clearly upset, maybe crying, but physically she looked well. I glanced around at all the sick women and wondered what was different about the woman in the white gown. What had she done that everyone else obviously wasn't prepared to do? The answer wasn't long in coming.

I started thinking back over the course of the year, from the moment I found out I was pregnant, all the way to the here and now. I'd been through so much that I was probably barely recognisable to my colleagues at work. I thought about the way things were before the Christmas party and my promotion. I imagined returning to those days, and a smile crossed my face. There was a way of achieving this without having to wait. I could go back to work, pick up where I'd left off and become my old self again. I could have all this if I did what the woman in the white gown had done. A termination would be the answer to all my problems.

When my time came to step into the doctor's office, it went so quickly that it hardly seemed worth it. I thought about mentioning the possibility of having a termination, but he didn't give me a chance. He just took one look at me, asked about my symptoms and said he'd increase my medication. Then a nurse escorted me to an awaiting taxi.

As soon as I stepped in through the front door, I felt an all-too-familiar churning sensation in my stomach. I had a couple of minutes before it became critical, so I tried to relax. I recalled what had passed through my mind earlier and how close I'd actually come to telling the doctor I wanted a termination. I was strong enough to resist the temptation then, so now, come what may,

I was determined to go through with it. And the first step towards achieving that was to try to picture myself holding a newborn baby in my arms. The hardship I was experiencing now would be more than worth it.

The month of November started in precisely the same vein. I didn't get better, but thankfully I didn't get any worse either. I was relying more and more on Femi to clean up after me. He did it begrudgingly, but without protestations to begin with. Then his attitude began to change. Whenever he came in, he just sighed and stormed off into the kitchen to get a cloth.

He made me feel so guilty, that I made more of an effort to run to the bathroom, but that only exacerbated things because I couldn't make it in time, and so left a trail of stains. Sometimes I did manage to get a cloth myself, but after a minute or two of scrubbing, I wanted to vomit again. I was only succeeding in making things worse.

It was while I was lying on the couch after a trip to the bathroom that I had an idea. I had been thinking a lot about the birth. Currently, we had no way of getting to the hospital in a manner that was timely, reliable or comfortable enough for a heavily pregnant woman. What we needed was a car.

So I managed to do some research on my laptop and found a Ford that I liked. Granted, it was nothing fancy, but it looked both robust and comfortable. Plus, after I had given birth I would want a way of getting around without too much trouble. It appeared to be the perfect solution, so a Ford it was going to be. And at only £4,000, the price fitted in with how much I wanted to spend. All that was left was to convince Femi. I was relying on him to buy it for me, and he wasn't going to do it unless he agreed with my decision.

"What, a Ford? You can't be serious."

"I am serious, Femi. I want something reliable and comfortable, nothing fancy. For our purposes, I don't think it's worth paying more than £4,000."

"But, answer me one thing. Are you an old woman?"

"No, I'm not, but—"

He ran an eye over me. "You are. That's what you've become. I am not buying a Ford."

"But Femi, I—"

He waved a hand. "I'm not buying a Ford, because I'm not an old man."

He turned away, mumbling to himself.

I thought about calling after him, but decided pretty quickly that it'd be pointless.

I pleaded with him again and again over the next few days. I even tried reasoning with him. I knew this would be pointless, but I thought I'd try anyway. So, I knew he wasn't going to buy a Ford, but for some reason I wasn't expecting him to go around splashing my cash the way he did.

He didn't buy a Ford; I was right. No, instead he came back with an Audi. He bought a bloody sports car with my money, putting his vanity above the practicalities. I felt like banging my head against the coffee table. I didn't have the strength to get angry with him.

Not feeling satisfied with this outrageous extravagance, he said that the car should be in his name. Of course, I protested, but he kept going on about it, over and over, getting angrier and angrier. So in the end I caved in.

It wasn't an easy decision, but one I had to make because the constant bickering was driving me insane.

Something changed in him this time around. I noticed he was increasingly angry, probably because he was sick of cleaning up after me. So, after each and every time I'd been sick, instead of lying down to recover, I went straight to the kitchen to get a cloth. That way I could relax in the knowledge that there wasn't going to be anything for him to be angry about. Sometimes things went according to plan, and other times I threw up again and made matters a whole lot worse.

On one occasion I didn't have the strength to clean up after myself, so I staggered back to the couch to sleep it off. When I awoke a couple of hours later, I took one look at the clock and set about scrubbing up the mess. I was only halfway through when the door opened. I could hear him seethe more and more with each step he took. When I could feel his breath on the back of my neck, I turned round to say hi, trying to sound as casual as possible. He took one look at the mess, and his eyes glazed over.

He deliberately sat where I was cleaning. I felt him leaning forwards, breathing down my neck. His boots started to creep towards me, leaving mud in the wet area I'd just cleaned. Then he lifted his foot, and for a moment I thought he had seen that he was making it awkward, so I allowed myself a smile of relief.

His boot dropped into the mess. I began scrubbing hard, as hard as I could, around the vicinity of his shoe, getting right in, trying my best to get under it. Then the next thing I knew, a sharp pain had engulfed the tops of my fingers. I yelped and accused him of doing it deliberately, in a jokey type of way. He just glared at me though. There was something sinister in his expression, something I hadn't seen before. I pushed myself up onto the couch and waited in silence for him to leave the room before I continued.

On to month eight of my pregnancy. The hyperemesis seemed to be getting worse in correlation to my size. I couldn't even get up for a wee without a struggle.

From that point onwards we couldn't even be in the same room without there being an argument. He was continually looking for a fight, bickering over the tiniest little thing, things that previously he'd just slipped in to make me feel bad. I couldn't cope with him any more and tried again to think of a way out. Then one day he came in, and his face was white. His eyes looked cold, kind of glazed over, as if he had been possessed by some sort of spirit. I smiled and said hi, but he didn't flinch. He took a step towards me. I looked at him, puzzled, wondering what the hell was going on. Then he whispered, "I'm going to kill you."

I'd heard him say this once before, and just like then, I got the feeling he meant it. Except that this time, it wasn't a threat; it was his intention. He put one foot in front of the other and lunged forwards. I moved my back against the couch, chin raised as far as it would go. Then he repeated, "I'm going to kill you."

My only chance was to stand up and try to make a run for it, to the safety of the bedroom, where I could lock myself away.

He stepped in front of me, blocking my path. "Femi, I—" He pulled back his arm to roughly 90 degrees. His fist clenched. His arm inched forwards. His mouth opened, and he screamed something inaudible. His fist dropped until it was in line with my stomach. It moved forwards until I could feel its heat like an approaching comet. The room went momentarily black. I wanted to scream, but the wind had been taken from me. My hand detached itself from my being and shot down towards the pain. I took a step back and made a noise that was unlike anything I'd heard before, or seen. His foot moved forwards, covering my ankles, then it swung in, sweeping me off my feet and sending me tumbling, head onto the floor.

I writhed around on the floor, holding my stomach, fighting to breathe, and trying to sit up to show him he couldn't beat me that easily. When I did manage to look up, I was just in time to see the door slam shut. The bang resounded around the house until it was drowned out by the sound of my own sobbing.

I lay there for some time clutching my stomach, cursing myself for not having the guts to leave him.

He kept a low profile for a few days after that, without ever hinting that he might try it again. I was living on eggshells though. Eventually, after three days, my friend Kemi came over. She immediately rushed towards me and asked what was wrong. I waited until he was out of earshot and then whispered. "He hit me a few days ago. Then he tripped me, and I fell." I gestured towards the patch of floor where it had happened.

Kemi was momentarily lost for words. "I'm going to confront him."

"No!"

She could be stubborn when she wanted to be, so I couldn't get through to her. As soon as he appeared, she smiled and told him to sit down. I wanted to stick my head between the floorboards and pretend I wasn't there. I fixed my gaze on the ceiling. I could hear them talking, but it was more like a distant mumbling sound, barely comprehensible through my self-made whirlwind. Then I heard her say, "She said you tripped her." And I came out of my trance.

"I tripped her? Oh no, she fell. She lost her balance, probably because she's expecting soon."

"Then why did she say you did?"

"I don't know. Because she's gone a bit..." He tapped his temple.

Kemi glanced at me through the corner of her eye and smiled at him, like she was communicating her thoughts non-verbally.

When I woke up the next morning, he wasn't there. I made it up onto my feet and took a look around. He was gone, and so too were some of his things. I retreated to the couch to try to solve the puzzle.

It took me almost an hour to walk to the shops that morning, which were just at the end of the street. It was a toil, but there was no alternative.

I bought something for dinner that night and a carton of orange juice. It was all I could manage. I had sweat dripping down my forehead by the time I was close enough to see in through the windows. My mouth tasted bitter from when I wanted to swallow a mouthful of sickness. I was just about to reach into my pocket and pull out the key when I noticed. The car had gone. I immediately put two and two together.

After struggling to put the groceries into the cupboard, I had a break before pouring myself some orange juice.

That's when it hit me; my boyfriend had left me and taken the car with him. I didn't know what I was going to do.

I was on my own, surrounded by vomit, getting bigger and bigger by the day. By that stage of my pregnancy, just standing up would have been an ordeal in itself, but my sickness compounded matters to make them far worse. Looking back, I can't believe I did this, but as each day passed, I hoped more and more that he'd come back. He might have gotten angry about having to clean the mess up, but I'd take that over having to do it myself any day of the week.

In December I gave birth to my first child, and although the pregnancy hadn't been easy, the minute I held her in my arms it all became worthwhile. My sister, Ayo, helped me a lot. She stayed with me those first few days after I went home, just to make sure I was OK. Then she had to go home, telling me to call her if I needed anything at all. I had to take things easy over the Christmas and New Year period, but I did manage to enjoy myself, thanks to the support network I had around me. To be honest, Femi's disappearance came as a bit of a relief. Who wouldn't feel relieved when they'd spent the last six months constantly bickering and walking on eggshells, having to be careful about everything they said. I was no longer feeling angry all the time, which felt like I had been released from prison.

No matter how much thought I gave to it, I couldn't work out why he'd done what he did. Not that I cared for his well-being; I was just curious to know. I had a fair idea of where he would have gone, probably with one of his friends or the other woman he had been seeing, who he thought I didn't know about. I continued to tell myself that being on my own was much better than living with someone who made me so unhappy.

Then one day, just after New Year, he breezed in, smiling, like he had been to the shops and brought me some orange juice. I managed to stave off my urge to ask him where he had been and why he had left me on my own to carry and give birth to his child. I did this because I knew it would just lead to hours of arguments that would end in me apologising and wishing I'd just kept my mouth shut to begin with.

I'd never been scared that he was going to hit me before that first time, but now it was an ever-present fear in my life. Every time we had an argument, his face went pale, and I knew then that I had gone too far. I tried not to be afraid, but the memory of his fist crashing into my stomach was still foremost in my mind. And now I had a daughter to look after too, so if something happened to me, she might end up with no one.

My friend was getting married around that time and had invited us both as a couple. I knew that for her sake I had to put on a brave face and pretend that everything was OK between us. At least that was my plan.

After the church ceremony, it was time for the reception. It was all going OK at first. We were chatting normally, enjoying the meal and generally having a good time. I was thinking how nice it was that we could enjoy a social occasion without bickering. Then I said something that he took exception to. I'm not sure what it was, but his face turned pale and his eyes glazed over. The signs were ominous.

I went to the Ladies, hoping that when I returned he would have calmed down and the situation would be diffused. My plan looked like it had been successful to start with. He smiled at me as I sat down next to him, but the minute I started talking, the glazed look was there again. This time, however, it was worse. Much worse. He looked possessed.

I couldn't make an excuse to go to the Ladies this time, so I pushed back my chair and said I was going to say hello to one of my friends who I hadn't seen for some time. I lifted my chair under the table and turned to walk away. Then I felt his hand wrapping around my arm.

I turned to protest, and he was there, his face a matter of inches from mine. He was as angry as I'd ever seen him. I stood rooted to the spot, eyeballing him, preparing myself, wondering where it was going to be this time. He raised his fist, pulled it back, aimed for my face and sent it hurtling towards me. I could feel the paralysing pain long before his clenched fist made contact. The next thing I knew, I was doubled over, my hands cupping my nose, standing in a puddle of my own blood.

My friend witnessed everything. She screamed, ran across, then told him to go away, which he did. Once I was stood up straight, she urged me to remove my hands so she could examine the damage. I refused to, but she kept on insisting until I bit the bullet and did as she'd asked. She took one look and called for an ambulance. Then she informed me she was calling the police. I protested, saying it was nothing really and that I was sure it wouldn't happen again, although I knew it was only a matter of time. Thankfully, she took no notice of me whatsoever.

The paramedics thought my nose was broken, which was later confirmed by a doctor. All I could think about, though, was my friend and how, if I had just kept my mouth shut, I wouldn't have ruined her day. I would never forgive myself.

Chapter Five
Motherhood, Baby, Abuse

It was a tough birth with few complications, which, I suppose, was something to be thankful for. I gave birth naturally too, without any anaesthetics.

I wasn't sure if the two were connected or not, but shortly after I gave birth, not that long after he returned, in fact, I started getting these unbearable migraines. And when I say unbearable, I mean unbearable. Sometimes they were so bad that I struggled to stand up to attend to my daughter, and when I did, I immediately clapped my hand across my forehead to try to soothe the throbbing pain.

I felt better momentarily when I held my daughter, but the minute I put her back in her cot, it returned. By the time I was back on the couch, it was so bad, I thought I was going to vomit. If I had vomited, it might have eased the pain, but I never did. I just continued to believe I was going to all the time. The only positive thing was that when my daughter cried, she never woke me up, because I was never asleep anyway. I couldn't sleep at night, and I struggled to sit up during the day. Even though I was a new mother, I sensed that this wasn't normal. And he was as useless as ever.

It was two weeks before I felt well enough to go to the chemist. I pushed my daughter along the pavement and observed how people smiled at me as they passed. The migraine had returned, and I found it hard to muster up a smile. I could tell that one old lady felt a bit put out when I didn't return the gesture. I know she meant well, but the last thing I needed was to stop and talk. I'm sure she would have understood.

So, with one hand on the pram and the other steadying myself on my neighbour's garden wall, I managed to make it to the pharmacy. As soon as I stepped inside, the woman who wore a white jacket rushed to my assistance. By the time I stood at the counter, she knew exactly what I needed. So I paid for the tablets and left the warm shop.

When I got home, it's safe to say that my migraine felt as bad as it ever did. I put my daughter back into her cot, made sure she was asleep and then ripped open the tablets the pharmacist had given me. When I'd set off earlier, I knew I would feel bad when I got home, but I presumed it would be short-term pain for long-term gain. Now I wasn't so sure if it was a worthwhile trade-off. An hour or so later, I decided it wasn't.

In desperation, I went into the bathroom and took out some shears. Ten minutes later I was back on the couch, hoping beyond hope that my drastic action would do the trick. Ten minutes after that, someone knocked.

"It's only me."

It was my friend Kemi. It was only once I felt a chill on my head that I started to panic. "Er, just one minute, Kemi. I'm not decent."

"Oh, OK, then."

I didn't like lying to her like that, but I had no choice if I was going to save my face. Fortunately, I had the perfect solution.

I started frantically searching around. I knew it was there, because I had seen it a few days earlier. I pulled out the wig and placed it on my head, hoping that it wasn't as skew-whiff as it had been on the newsreader I'd seen recently.

Kemi had had her baby around the same time as me, so she paid frequent visits to show me how her daughter was doing and to get updates on mine. I wanted to go round to hers too, but it was hard, what with my migraines and all. She understood.

She knew where everything was, so she went into the kitchen to make us both a drink while I kept an eye on the children.

As soon as I reached out to take the cup, I noticed the way she was looking at me. "Excuse me a minute." I got to my feet. "Quick call of nature." She nodded to say she understood.

This was another lie. Facing the mirror in the bathroom, I removed my wig. I was totally bald, with one or two scratches that suddenly felt sore. I thought about putting it back on, but I knew I couldn't keep up the pretence to one of my oldest friends.

As soon as I opened the door, I knew it was a mistake. She was attending to her baby before she looked over her shoulder. I could tell she was about to say something before she gasped. I wanted the ground to open up and swallow me. I marched straight to the couch, hoping that my attempts to avoid eye contact were not too conspicuous. As soon as my head hit the back of the chair, I sighed. Whatever it was that I had just seen in the mirror, it definitely wasn't the same person I was a few months earlier.

"Tinuke, what's happened to your—"

"Just leave it, please."

"What is it?" Kemi reached across and patted my leg. At any other time, I'd have basked in such a warm and compassionate gesture, but I wished she'd go away and leave me. I shrugged. "Oh, it's nothing."

Kemi persisted. "You sure?" Anything to avoid the elephant in the room.

I nodded. "Yeah." I turned to look at her baby. "Doing well, isn't she? Looks like her mum."

Kemi beamed. "Yeah, she's grown a lot though, already. I was on the phone to the pastor yesterday, to book her christening."

"Any luck?"

"Yeah. It's going to be in the summer. July."

I imagined the warm sunshine on my face. "That sounds good, Kemi. I'll look forward to that."

Kemi smiled, but made no further comment on the subject.

Kemi and her husband, Bayo, were close friends of mine. We'd known each other for years, after meeting at church. They were delighted when I'd first met Femi and were eager to meet him. He then became close to both of them, just like me, but mostly close to Bayo. I wasn't sure how I felt about this. It sometimes felt as if he had muscled in on my friendship, and they had forgotten about me, whom they've known for years.

They were both solicitors and had an office about five minutes away. So it was easy for us to meet up after work and enjoy a drink and a chat. This was great at first, although I did not enjoy having to pretend we were the perfect couple to them. As an outsider looking in, it appeared to me that they were the perfect couple too, but who knows what was happening when they were alone together. For all I knew, Kemi could have been going through the same thing as I was.

Things began to turn sour not long after I introduced Femi to them. He and Bayo hit it off straight away and arranged to go for a drink together. When I first heard about this, I did feel a bit sceptical, but then I told myself that Bayo would keep him out of trouble. Unlike Femi, he was a sensible, mature adult, who would be a good influence. So, after a brief moment of hesitation, I told them both it was a great idea and to have a nice time. Since then, it became a recurring theme of conversation whenever it was just Kemi and me. So I knew exactly what her next words were going to be.

"Now, Tinuke."

I smiled, trying to give the impression that I didn't know where she was going.

"Bayo has been telling me a few things that Femi told him."

Once again, I cursed the day I ever let them go for a drink together. "Really?"

"Yes, and… well…"

"Well, what?"

"Oh, nothing. Forget about it."

"No, I won't forget about it. Tell me what he said."

"OK then. He said you've been neglecting your duties as a woman."

I couldn't be bothered to fake surprise this time. "How?"

"He said, well, for one thing, you haven't been looking after yourself."

This still took the wind out of me, even though I fully expected her to say it. I just shrugged and shook my head.

"Tinuke, don't be like that. I—"

"What do *you* think? Do you think I've let myself go?"

"No, of course I don't. I'd say that considering everything..."

I diverted my thoughts elsewhere. It was obvious she did agree, but was just trying to skirt around the subject. We spent the next few minutes in silence, separated by an impenetrable wall of awkwardness. "It's time this little one was fed," I said, getting to my feet.

She took the hint. "Oh, well, I'll be off then."

Whenever she came to visit over the following months, this barrier existed between us, although neither of us said anything. I could tell she was thinking about it though. Every time she looked at me, it was there, written all over her face. I knew if I mentioned it, she would imply that it was all in my imagination, especially as she'd never come right out and said I'd let myself go to begin with. I felt the need for constant reassurance, which I never got from Femi.

On one occasion, when the phone rang, I sighed, reached over and pushed the green button. It was Kemi. I spent ten minutes or so conversing, then I started to feel tired. But however much I tried, I couldn't get rid of her. She just kept on talking, filling up every break in the conversation with drivel until exasperation took hold of me. It came as a huge relief when she said her daughter needed feeding and she had to go. Maybe this was an excuse to get away, but I felt relieved nonetheless. From then on, I felt reluctant to pick the phone up when anyone rang. Sometimes I'd just pretend I wasn't there. They often kept on ringing though, so in the end I had to answer just so they'd go away.

Somehow I managed to get through until July, when, for a while, I started looking forward to Kemi's christening. I kept on looking on the Internet, trying to figure out what I was going to wear and how I was going to have my hair cut, but as the time approached, my enthusiasm waned. On the day before, I just wanted to be left alone.

I got up with good intentions, but as soon as I stepped out of the bathroom, I just couldn't be bothered. I looked at the clothes from my previous existence, now bunched together at the end of my wardrobe, and then imagined how tight they'd be. I had put on a lot of weight since I'd last worn them. So instead I pulled out a comfortable skirt and jumper from my drawer. I didn't look in the mirror once.

As soon as I stepped into the crowded room, I knew everyone was looking at me. They smiled and said hi as I passed, but I knew what they were thinking. They were thinking that I looked a mess and were wondering why I hadn't bothered making any effort. I regretted not looking in the mirror earlier on. I felt so ashamed, that I couldn't make eye contact with anyone, least of all people I had known for years. I could hear them whispering about me behind my back.

Bayo's face was the first friendly face I saw. He and Femi had been thick as thieves, but he was still a nice guy, that much I did know. So I sidled up to him and murmured, "Bayo, tell me honestly, do I look OK?" I waited with bated breath for his reply, wishing I had omitted the bit about honesty.

"Yes, Tinuke, of course you do. You look divine in that skirt."

Thankfully, he'd read my thoughts. I flashed him a grin, just to acknowledge the gesture, and turned away. What I saw was a crowd of happy, friendly people. They were still looking at me, but this time they seemed friendly. I smiled back at them, and as I did so, I started to worry that I had been imagining things before. So when I overheard Femi whispering about me to Bayo, I thought I might have lost my marbles.

"Femi, my friend, I'd like to compliment you on how dapper you look."

"Why, thank you."

Bayo glanced at me over his shoulder. "But what about Tinuke? Why would you let your wife come dressed like that? Why didn't you tell her?"

"Because, she wouldn't have listened. She's like that all the time now." He pulled out a picture from his wallet. "Here, have a look at this."

Bayo took the photo and held it up to eye level.

"Can you believe it's the same woman?"

Bayo shook his head. "Nah. She's let herself go big time, hasn't she?"

Femi nodded. "Yeah. It's a real turnoff in the bedroom department, I can tell you."

Bayo laughed. "Well, I'd get a shot for that reason alone."

I took my daughter from the pram and retreated to a corner to feed her. I breastfed her, which attracted even more disgusted looks.

By the time it was time for us to leave, I was sitting in a corner on my own. It was just like I was a hired help who was invited to the ceremony as a token gesture. I couldn't wait to get back home so I could hide away in my own thoughts, where I was untouchable by the outside world.

As soon as I removed my coat, I sunk down into the couch and dropped my chin into my hands. I was determined not to subject myself to that kind of humiliation again. Next time someone invited me somewhere, I was going to politely refuse.

This resolve was soon put to the test when another friend invited me to her engagement party. Recalling the promise I'd made to myself, I avoided answering, until I was able to just slip it into the conversation that I wasn't going to go. She made out she was OK with this, but I could tell she wasn't. She rang back the next day, but I didn't answer. I chose to let her go on worrying about me rather than talk to her and have to explain myself over and over. I just couldn't be bothered. All I had to look forward to was going back to work.

I opened the office doors and entered, finding I was the first to arrive. I'd been looking forward to this day for some time, so nothing could dampen my enthusiasm. As soon as my desktop PC started flashing, I tried to imagine how the coming eight hours would unfold. I glanced down at my skirt, which was much tighter and generally more uncomfortable than I remembered.

Everyone professed to be pleased to see me. All my old friends rushed over to say hi and catch up on my news. They all wanted to know about my daughter. I was just as interested to hear their news too, so everyone gathered around my desk for ten minutes until my boss walked in. The crowd immediately dispersed, giving her a clear line of vision to look at me and say it was nice to have me back. I said it was good to be back, and I meant it. I really did.

For the first time in ages I had a reason to get out of bed each morning. I started sleeping better too, and little by little, felt my old self coming back to the fore.

Towards the end of September, Femi and I started thinking about our own engagement. We talked and talked about every little detail. I felt that, after such a challenging year, this was what I needed to cement my place back in the land of the living. Femi, though, soon reverted back to type.

Each time I suggested we do some research into possible venues, he made up some excuse to get away. He was convincing as always, so I went along and started the process. Then I got suspicious, so I had it out with him. He told me he was just as interested as I was and that I was imagining things—again. From that moment on, he showed no interest at all; in fact, he didn't even mention it again. So I had the choice of organising everything myself or not having an engagement party at all. I knew that if I didn't take on the responsibility, I might live to regret it.

I was happy to do this, and when he said he'd give me half the money back, I approached the task with some relish. Once it was all booked and paid for, I asked about the money. He just made his excuses and walked away. When I was younger, I never imagined that I'd have to pay for my own engagement party. That's just not the way things are supposed to work. All in all, the party cost me £15,000.

Chapter Six
Pregnancy and abuse

I left the comfort of the couch to look through the window, stopping about an inch or so from the ledge. I placed a hand over the bubble on my stomach and cast my mind back to my previous pregnancy.

Despite everything that had happened back then—the physical and psychological abuse, being ostracised by the Nigerian community etc.—it was the sickness that I remembered most vividly. It had thought it was a cross I'd always have to bear, but fortunately I was spared this time. And for the moment, there was no sign of physical abuse either.

I glanced up at the clock. I'd been standing there, lost in my thoughts and hadn't realised how hungry I had become. I pulled out a box of porridge oats that were right at the front of the cupboard and put a sachet in the microwave for a couple of minutes. It tasted good, washed down with a glass of Fanta.

I was still at work at this time, but my maternity leave was approaching fast. My boss was supportive, but I could tell she was a bit put out. I remember the look on her face when I first told her. She faked the kind of smile that suggested she was anything but happy.

A month or so later, I was sitting staring through the window on a Wednesday afternoon. I inhaled the smell of freshly cut grass. There were people outside wearing light jackets, or in some cases no jacket at all. I didn't have to look at the calendar to know that summer was on the way. Soon, God willing, I'd be able to go out for a walk, maybe to the park. I imagined the warm sunshine on my face and smiled.

The weather in the UK varies greatly. It's either roasting, freezing, pouring with rain or absolutely perfect. And this summer fell into the latter category. It was August, and I couldn't remember my spirits being so high.

Wearing a t-shirt and a light pair of pants, I got Funmilola, my daughter, ready for a trip out to the nearby swings. But I needed something to salivate in before I could go anywhere. I dropped an old Lucozade bottle into my bag. This was so I could use the orange wrapping to conceal its contents.

There was another woman already there with her kid. Her child was younger than Funmi, about one. Despite her friendly greeting, it was clear that she would rather be on her own too. As soon as she heard the scrunching sound of the Lucozade wrapper, she gave me a disapproving look and stormed off. My disbelief didn't even last a minute before I basked in the solitude.

That afternoon stands out in my mind because the weather was delightful. In the trees opposite, squirrels scurried around, and the wood pigeons hooted. I had no idea how long I was sat there contemplating before I glanced down at Funmi and saw that she was getting a bit tired. So, reluctantly, I made my way home.

That was the night he informed me that his friend from Nigeria was getting married and told me to find something decent to wear.

It was always tricky using the Underground while I was pregnant. This time, however, I didn't mind. I had to stand by the door, but then some gallant gentlemen took pity on me and offered me his seat, which I graciously accepted. I still had to breathe in the hot, grimy air, though, which made me feel increasingly nauseous.

I enjoyed that afternoon. I had to choose something from the maternity department, but even that didn't dampen my spirits.

I was still in a good mood when I took it (my dress) from the bag and held it to the window when I got home. I even managed a short laugh when I thought about how, in a previous life, I wouldn't have been seen dead in something as frumpy as this.

I showed it to him when he came in, doing my best to put a positive spin on it. He took one look and walked away, mumbling to himself.

A couple of weeks later, the big day arrived. However, the minute I got out of bed, I knelt over. I ran to the bathroom to be sick, which made me feel a hundred times better, but I was too weak to put on a show. So I told him I wasn't feeling well enough to attend.

He cast his eyes at the floor and shook his head. Then he inched his head upwards until he was looking right at me. His eyes glazed over. This was going to be bad, but I could tell that he wouldn't hurt me physically.

He raised his chin and shouted so loud that I had to cover my ears. He went on and on about how I always embarrass him and how he was going to be the butt of everyone's jokes. I tried to protest, saying that people would understand, but he wouldn't listen. In a fit of rage, he took hold of a chair, raised it to eye level and threw it onto the floor. I was scared. But, to my relief, he turned around and left without saying another word.

I glanced at the clock and calculated how much time I had before he came back inebriated and eager for a fight. I didn't want to sit down and waste the day clock-watching, so I decided to visit the Westfield Centre instead. I ate a bowl of porridge, drank a glass of Fanta and left the house, wearing my posh dress and a smile. I wasn't going to be beaten that easily.

I enjoyed my excursion, but it was overshadowed by a feeling of impending doom. I tried to kid myself that, because I was in such high spirits, all I had to do was stay positive. By the time I arrived home, I had convinced myself. That was about 7 pm. Four hours later, I was expecting the worst.

My eyelids felt heavy. I knew he wouldn't be happy if he came back to find me asleep in bed, so I put something on YouTube to try to keep myself awake. It didn't work.

The door slammed, and his pounding footsteps headed towards me. I rubbed my eyes and managed to muster up a smile.

"Hi, did you have a nice time?" I said, trying to make my smile look as natural as possible.

"You made me a laughing stock." He went into the bedroom to change out of his smart clothes, cursing under his breath.

He was calm, to begin with. He started telling me about his friends, but then moved on to a conversation he'd had about one of my friends.

"She has an interesting past, doesn't she?"

"Interesting? In what way?"

"All the men she's had. She likes to sleep around a bit, doesn't she?"

"No. I don't know what—"

He started slurring his words. "Sounds promiscuous to me."

"No, she's a—"

"What I want to know is, why are you friends with her? You must be promiscuous too. Have you been sleeping around behind my back?"

I knew that whatever I said, he wasn't going to believe me, so just to avoid all the bickering, I shrugged and shook my head.

His eyes glazed over. "I'll take that as a yes then, shall I?"

I saw the crazed monster he turns into when he's about to get violent. I had a young daughter asleep in her bedroom. I had to protect her at all costs. I couldn't leave her at his mercy. I made a dash for the bedroom door.

His fingers dug into the fleshy part of my upper arm, midway between my shoulder and my elbow.

"No, please." Gritting my teeth, I strengthened my grip around the door handle and attempted to open it.

He pulled me back, stretching my arm to breaking point. I fell back, lost my balance and crashed onto the floor. My mothering instinct kicked in, making me wrap my arms around my stomach, protecting my unborn Child Tomi was the first thing that came to mind. Desperate to conceal my distress, I started to push myself up, looking right through him with a steely determination.

His open hand headed towards my face, his fingers as wide apart as they could go. The heel of his hand tilted towards me, his palm straightened and his fingers bent. I caught a whiff of the soap we used in the bathroom. His fingers turned the other way and... my lips slammed into my teeth. I felt the blood pooling in my nose long before the fingers on my forehead. But he wasn't done yet.

He pushed my head back, moved his other hand over my head and took a fistful of hair. I screamed and moved my hand to my nose. Something soft but bony slammed into my forehead, pushing my head backwards. The back of my head slammed into the floor, shrouding my entire body in pain. He grabbed another fist full of hair, pulled me towards him then hit my head back down into the floor. The process repeated over and over, until I thought my skull was about to break under the pressure of his hand.

He pulled my head back until my chin was raised far enough for me to look into his eyes. His arm moved back just past his elbow and his hand clenched into a fist. I struggled in vain to shake him off, and then closed my eyes, now knowing where the blow would land.

My eye became a ball of agony, my eyelid seemingly glued down to stop the pain from spreading. He exhaled through his nose. He threw his arm forwards, his fist approaching like a caveman's club being shot from a gun. This time I knew full well where it was going to land.

His grip tightened around my hair. He moved his arm back. Again, I sensed his fist hurtling towards me through my screwed-up eye. I gritted my teeth, swallowed my pain and waited for the next blow, and the next, and the next.

I let out a scream that must surely have been heard halfway along the street. Maybe someone would hear and come to my aid, unaware that they'd be putting themselves at risk.

My daughter. I had to get up, make sure she was OK and not too terrified to move. Her bedroom door opened. "Mummy."

At this point I was writhing around on my side, one hand on my bubble and the other over my eye. I sat up, feeling too ashamed to look her in the eye. "Mummy," she said again, stepping towards me. With his breath on the back of my neck, I heaved myself to my knees and opened my arms. Tears were streaming down her cheeks.

I turned to look at him with what must have been the most pathetic of expressions, to try to predict his next move. I had stopped caring about myself. He could hit me all he liked and nothing would make any difference. While in this state of mind, he was capable of anything; he could do to her what he had just done to me. "No, please," I mumbled, just as I had earlier. This time there was no shame. I was just looking out for my daughter. I hugged her again, both eyes screwed this time. We were still hugging when the door slammed. It was over.

I continued to hug Funmi, my thoughts drifted to her little brother Tomi inside me, praying and hoping he was ok, just then I felt him kick, each of us with tears dripping down our necks. I tapped on her back and told her she had to go back to bed. She protested, said she wasn't tired, then I took hold of her hand, and she placed it on my belly to feel the little kicks, and she smiled, I smiled back and drifted to sleep.

We sat there talking for about half an hour. I wanted to try to give her the impression that everything was OK, and there was nothing for her to worry about. I asked her about nursery, what she had been doing and her new friends. She told me all about it. When she went back to sleep, I left her room, fully intending to go to bed myself, but I couldn't muster up the strength. Instead I dropped onto the chair and thought things through. It had all happened so quickly that it wasn't even 2 am yet. I sunk my chin into my hands.

By the time I looked up, it was past 7 am. Suddenly overcome by tiredness, I sat back and closed my eyes. A bullet of pain shot from my eye to my cheekbone. Despite being shattered, I was in too much pain to sleep, so I decided to call my mum.

She demanded to know why I was calling her at that time. I just told her I'd had a row with Femi and couldn't sleep thinking about it. She was sympathetic and suggested I go over to see her. I thought about it for five minutes before going into Funmi's room to get the poor little mite out of bed.

I lived in East London, Canning Town, and my mum in Shepherd's Bush in the West. So, what with all the changing and waiting around, it took well over an hour to get there.

At Stratford I found a bench and sat down. I turned to look at Funmi. She was falling asleep, so I lifted her onto my lap. Next thing I knew I felt hot breath on my head. I swung round, squeezing my eyes shut under my dark glasses and clutching Funmi as tight as I dared without hurting her. It's fair to say that I've never felt so relieved to see a police officer in my life.

"Are you OK, madam?"

Madam? No one had called me that in a while. "Oh, yes, I'm fine."

"You don't look it. Let me see your eye"

I wished he'd go back to wherever he'd just come from—the station or something. "It looks a lot worse than it feels."

The policeman gave it some thought. "Pardon me, madam, but I'm not sure I believe you. Are you sure you're OK—I mean you haven't been a victim of domestic abuse, have you?"

I stuttered before replying. "I… er… no. Like I said, everything's fine."

"So you don't want to report anything then? Nothing at all?"

"No. Thank you."

I don't know why I said that. It certainly wasn't because I felt sorry for him, nor was it out of a misplaced sense of loyalty. No, I suppose it was because I hadn't thought about it. I wasn't feeling up to making a decision that would have far-reaching consequences, so it was easier just to do nothing. I got the feeling, though, that after I had given it some thought, and when my head had cleared, I might just change my mind.

The Underground was packed out by that time. The crowds were for our five deep at the doors, which meant I had to let the first train go and hope the next wouldn't be all that long in coming. By the time I had a clear view of the track, I was so hot and bothered that I actually enjoyed the gust of dirty air produced by a passing train.

When I finally stepped onto the train, surprise, surprise, there wasn't a spare seat to be found. I scanned the aisle, trying to make eye contact with anyone who looked like he might be a gentleman. A minute or so later a man wearing a grey mac over smart grey trousers got up to offer me his seat.

My mum lived about five minutes' walk from Shepherd's Bush station, but on that August morning it felt more like five hours. I pushed open the front door and stepped inside. She was in the kitchen, busy cooking something, probably my breakfast. I hoped beyond hope that it was porridge and that for some strange reason she had a massive bottle of Fanta in the fridge.

I removed my dark glasses, and a sticky river flowed down my cheek. I wiped it away with the back of my hand.

Chapter Seven
Betrayal by Family

It wasn't porridge, and she didn't have any Fanta, but I enjoyed breakfast anyway. The world looked strange through the dark glasses I had perched on my nose. Each time my jaws clenched, I winced, which made the glasses slide further and further down my nose. I didn't have the strength to keep on adjusting them, so I had to curl my nose to stop them falling off into my breakfast.

My mum took out her phone. "I don't like the look of this Tinuke, not one bit. I'm phoning your sister, to hear what she says."

My first thoughts were that it was a bit early on in the morning to be bothering her, but there was no point in protesting. Then I thought about it some more and felt my spirits rise.

"Oh my God!" My sister, Ayo, brushed past my mum. "Look at you. What on earth…"

I wasn't feeling well enough for this conversation, so I just shrugged. Her husband gave me a close examination and insisted I go to hospital.

My eyes felt bad when we set off for Charing Cross Hospital, and the journey made it worse. Each time the car ran over a divot or an uneven patch of road, a bolt of pain shot upwards, making me wince and cry out in pain. My sister's husband had examined me through dark glasses, so when the doctor gasped and fetched a mirror, it came as a great shock to us both. It felt like I had been smacked with a club, so I was expecting a lot of bruising. I wasn't expecting it to look anywhere near as bad as it did. I worried that I might be disfigured for life.

The doctor could only offer me sympathy and a prescription for painkillers. He said to keep my dark glasses on and to go to my GP if things took a turn for the worse.

I couldn't open my eye at all. A disgusting yellow liquid poured from the corner, and the pain was so bad that my entire head throbbed. The area stretching from the corner of my eye to my jaw was the worst. Each time I tried to open my eyes or chew, it felt like someone was hitting me with a hammer.

My mum came with me on the Underground back to East London. As soon as I opened the door and took a look round, the events of the previous night replayed in my mind. Although he wasn't there, and didn't wear a distinctive scent, I could smell him. The dishes were still on the rack, and his dirty glass was on the table.

My mum stayed with me as long as I needed her. She took care of Funmi and did the cooking, which made me feel a whole lot better. My eye aside, I enjoyed having someone run around after me for a change. It had been a while since anyone had taken care of me.

I followed the doctor's instructions to the letter, took painkillers and wore dark glasses all the time, but the swelling never seemed to go down. And the disgusting sticky stuff kept on coming. As soon as I dabbed it away with a tissue, it came again. My mum kept fetching me a fresh swab every few minutes and put those I'd already used in the bin. Funmi had been through enough already. The last thing I wanted was for her to see pieces of cotton wool everywhere, screwed up and crusty with the puss from her mother's eye.

We went back to A&E. This time, I was referred to the eye hospital, where I went a few days later. The specialist was like a dog with a bone.

"What happened to you then, Tinuke?"

"I tripped and fell over."

"Come on."

I hesitated. "Honestly, that's what happened."

The specialist shook her head. She was a no-nonsense sort of woman who wouldn't have looked out of place in a matron's uniform. I refused to tell her, but she wouldn't let it drop.

"It was my husband."

"Hmm. I thought so. I've seen it a million times before. "What was the trigger?"

"He wanted me to go with him to his friend's wedding. I said I would, but then when it came round, I didn't feel well enough to go."

The specialist nodded. "Tinuke, listen to me. You have to tell the police about this."

"But—"

"No buts. You have to stop him from doing it again." She glanced down at Funmi, who was sitting quietly on a chair. "Next time, it might be your daughter."

But my mum was against the idea.

"No, don't do anything hasty, will you?"

"No, I won't, but—"

"Do you want your children to grow up without a father? To be treated as outcasts and have to live off scraps?"

"No, I don't but—"

"Well, let it drop then. No good will come of it if you go blabbing to the police. Honestly, you don't know how lucky you are."

Lucky?

"Millions of women go through this, or worse. If they went blabbing to the police every time…"

I couldn't believe that my own mother was siding with him, and not her own flesh and blood.

She had a point though. The last thing I wanted was for Funmi to grow up without her father on the scene, but I didn't want him to get away with it either. It was a tough decision.

I had to go for laser treatment every two weeks, and to an extent it worked. My retina had been severely damaged. They weren't sure if it was ever going to get better. So I had to continue to wear dark glasses when exposed to intense light and just hope for the best.

I told the police. I decided that if I kept my mouth shut and played the good little wife, I'd be putting Funmi at risk. So they put out a search party for him, and the next day I got a phone call to say that they had found him.

Before all this happened, we'd been seeing the pastor at NMC Church for some marriage counselling. I wasn't sure if it actually achieved anything, but it was good to have someone to talk to. Just getting it out in the open made things much better. They wanted me to pay him a visit. I was reluctant to see him at first, but my family insisted. They said I'd be safe, as the pastor wouldn't let him harm me, and when my sister's husband said he'd go with me, I agreed.

It still came as a shock to see him sitting there wearing a smile stretching from one side of his face to the other. He was talking to the pastor like they were bosom buddies. When they burst out laughing at something I couldn't quite make out, my sister's husband joined in. I was determined to hold my own, despite being outnumbered three to one.

The pastor was still grinning when he asked for my version of events. I could tell by his demeanour that he wasn't taking me seriously. When I finished talking, he leant forward and asked me to remove my glasses. I did as he asked, then I winced and my hand shot up over my eye. The pastor insisted I move my hand, so I did. Femi just stared at the ceiling, like it didn't concern him at all. I was relieved that he didn't laugh though, because if he had...

"Tinuke, you have to take him back," the pastor said with an air of authority.

I shook my head.

"You have to. This is the Devil's work, don't you see? Marriage is a sacred sacrament, which shields you from the Devil's work. He wants to split you up so he can do his worst. If you don't do this, then you'll have to suffer the consequences. You have a wonderful daughter. Everyone in the church admires you. Do you really want to disappoint everyone and put yourself at the mercy of the Devil?"

I didn't know what to think or say. I was sitting in the presence of a man of God, who had just told me to forgive a man who had beaten me to a point where I might not see again. His logic made no sense at all.

The pastor sighed then turned to him.

"Femi, you've been sitting there waiting patiently for your wife to have her say. Now it's your turn. Let's hear your version of events."

The pastor sat back and made himself comfortable.

"Pastor, we were due to go to my friend's wedding. Then on the day, she changed her mind. They're good people, and I told her this, but she wouldn't listen. She doesn't care about anyone but herself."

The pastor nodded. "Some people have to be the centre of attention. It's the Devil's work."

"I got talking to a decent man, who is highly reputable. He said he knew one of Tinuke's friends and told me all about her. Pastor, she is a highly promiscuous woman. When I got home, I told all this to Tinuke. I was distressed at the thought that she might be promiscuous too, or else why would they be friends?"

The pastor nodded.

"She should have listened to what I said and made me see that she wasn't like that. But... she gave me no such assurances. She sided with this promiscuous woman— with the Devil—and it made me angry. Any decent man would have acted the same way."

"I understand all this, and in many ways you are right. But you shouldn't have woken her. And you need to stop drinking, because that's the Devil's work too."

"Yes, I'm being punished. I'm being punished for the way she has broken our sacred bond. But it wasn't like how she said."

"How was it then?"

"She slapped me first. She slapped me, so I hit her back. Is that wrong? Isn't that what any man with an ounce of self-respect would have done?"

The pastor nodded before shooting me a quick glance. "Son, you are right. She has issued an invitation to the Devil, and he has responded. You are being punished for your wife's misgivings. You were right to hit her. Son, I would have done exactly the same thing if it were my wife."

I couldn't take it anymore. Holy man or not, I had had enough. So I got up and stormed out.

The pastor didn't try to stop me. He just called out in a thick Nigerian accent, "Tinuke, if he ever does anything like this again, you just call me, OK?"

I kept on walking without turning back.

My sister's husband ran after me and told me to get into his car so he could take me home.

"It's just not fair," I muttered under my breath. "It's like there's one rule for men and another for women." I wanted to add, *What kind of church condones this?* But kept this to myself.

I sat staring through the windscreen without turning my head or uttering a single word. He hadn't said a word in my defence, so in my view, he was just as bad. And as for the pastor, I'd had it. As far as I was concerned the church stank, and I was never going back.

My mum and brother were waiting when I got back.

"What the—" It came as a great shock to my brother, who hadn't seen the damage before. "Wait till I see him," he glowered and shook his head. "I'll break his neck, that's what I'll do."

My mum said, "No. There'll be no violence from anyone. That won't do any good at all. You'll just make everything worse and land yourself in trouble while you're at it."

I kicked off my shoes and tried to make sense of it all. I had made a few hasty decisions earlier, and I had assumed that once I calmed down I'd change my mind. But the more I thought back, the angrier I became. No, I was never going to trust in that pastor again. And what's more, I'd had it with the church. I was never going back.

A car pulled up outside. I knew straight away, from the sound of the engine, that it was him. Sure enough, the car door thudded, and he got out. He was on the phone to someone, bickering. The doorbell rang.

"How dare you?" I said, blocking the entrance to the house. I could hear my brother stand up, and my mum telling him not to interfere.

"If you could just let me talk to you. Come on, do as the pastor said. You know it makes sense."

I stood firm. "How dare you do this to me and come over here."

"So, let's get this right. You're refusing me entry into my own house?"

"It's not *your* house."

"My marriage then."

"That's right. Not until—"

"Fine, if that's the way you want to play it." He turned his back on me.

It had been too easy; I didn't trust him. "What! Where are you going?"

"The pastor, Tinuke, the pastor. I can't wait to hear what he has to say about this."

"Fine."

I closed the door and went back inside to my family. My mum was deep in thought. "Did you, Tinuke?"

"Did I what?"

"Slap him? Slap him first?"

I sighed. "Oh, no. How could I?"

"You could very well—"

"No, Mum, I couldn't. I was living off Fanta and porridge. I had no energy to hit anyone. Honestly."

My mum nodded. "He's been lying about you to everyone, Tinuke."

"I know."

"You need to get him to write it down, admit it and be a man for once."

This was a good idea, but it meant having to see him again, which I didn't really want to do. "I will, next time I see him."

For the next couple of days everything was quiet. So quiet that I was starting to think he had been bluffing. Then, right out of the blue, my sister's husband showed up. He brushed past me without saying a word and sat on the couch, on the middle seat. "Come on," he said, patting the seat next to him.

Any other time I'd be offended at the way he was acting like the host in my own home, but on this occasion I didn't have the energy. It didn't feel right sitting next to him though, so I pulled up a wooden dining chair and sat opposite him, with my back to the TV.

I got tired of listening to him breathe. "Well?"

"I've had word from your pastor." My sister's husband was also a pastor. That's why he often got snippets of things before they were made common knowledge.

I sighed. "Well?"

"He went back to see the pastor—"

"Yeah, he said he would."

"And didn't have much positive to say about you. In fact, I'd say you are a stubborn woman who doesn't know what's right for her and her child."

Again, I didn't have the energy to be indignant. "Would you now?"

"Tinuke, I know you've had your problems, but your standards are too high. Just look around you; I can't see anyone rushing to be with you, can you?"

"I don't have high standards. I just want to be treated like a human being, that's all."

"Your standards are too high, and you need to see your true station in life. Until you do that, then..."

He stood up to leave.

"Then what?"

"I'm washing my hands of you, Tinuke. There's nothing more I, or anyone else, can do until you accept your situation."

A dark cloud descended and took away my courage. "But, what if—he could come back and I'll be on my own. He could kill me this time."

He looked at me over his shoulder on his way out.

Chapter Eight
With or Without You

June 2017

Things had been going OK since Tomi was born in January. I wouldn't say I was feeling on top of the world, but I was more positive than I had been for a long time. Femi wasn't that bad either, which led me to think that maybe our troubles had all been down to my negative vibes.

We started going out for a few days, but I soon realised the car wasn't suitable for a family. It was on the tip of my tongue to suggest we sell the Audi, which he had chosen, but I didn't want to spoil things. The problem was, I could see how uncomfortable the children were, so I had no choice but to take matters into my own hands.

I did some research on the Internet and found a car dealership nearby that would take the Audi in part exchange for a Countryman, which was a car I'd always wanted.

I was only a couple of seconds into my test drive when I decided it was the car for me, and I left the dealership with a huge smile on my face. The minute I stepped back into the house, however, I started clock watching.

I had to tell him before he saw for himself. "Femi, I've sold the Audi."

"You've what?"

"I've sold the Audi. We needed a car more suitable for a family, I know you chose it but—"

"OK, that's fine. I agree. Whatever you say."

I opened my mouth, but no words would come.

At last I had bought something for myself that he approved of. Maybe he was changing.

Trouble was, because it was a family car, no one saw it as being my own personal asset. He took it out almost every day, leaving me stuck inside gazing through the window. This could have put me back down in the doldrums, but I was determined not to let it bother me. Things between us were good, and I wanted to keep it that way.

I told all this to my brother, who was delighted for me. He was somewhat concerned that Femi was taking the car I'd bought for myself, but I managed to persuade him it was OK. Then he went and spoiled it. "What about the money for your engagement party? Wasn't he meant to be paying you half of it back?"

I'd put this to the back of my mind. "Yes, he was, but—"

"But he hasn't. He has to. You do know that, don't you?"

"Yes."

"I have an idea."

"Oh, what's that?"

I'm starting this new venture, I told you about it, didn't I?"

"Yeah."

"I need some delivery men so—this is up his street isn't it?"

I smiled at the pun. "Yeah, but he's working for Amazon."

"No, problem; he can work whenever."

I smiled. "Great."

My brother waited with me for him to come in, and when he did, he accepted the job with some relish. My brother and I exchanged glances.

I told him right away to concentrate on his jobs and not to worry about coming home to help out with the errands, which he appreciated.

My brother was something of a fitness fanatic at the time, so he had contacts in the industry. The first delivery Femi was assigned, therefore, was to my brother's personal trainer. Protein powders, energy drinks, protein bars, supplements, that kind of thing.

Everything went well. With his Amazon job as well, I hardly ever saw him. Whenever he came home late, he slept on the couch so he wouldn't disturb me and the kids. Well, that's why I thought he did it anyway.

I started to become a bit suspicious of his motives. He just came in and made himself comfortable without saying a word. Sometimes I was awake. I coughed or made other noises, but he never came in, which I thought was really strange. Once I called out, and when he still didn't come in to see me, I knew there was something wrong.

The next night I held my breath, and lo and behold, he was talking to someone on the phone. I got up to see who he was talking to, and when he saw me, he gave me the same embarrassed look I knew only too well.

He muttered his goodbyes, shoved his phone in his pocket and smiled at me, as if nothing was wrong. It was like he thought I was too stupid to work out what he was up to. There was a moment of awkward silence while I thought about what to do. In the end I decided not to go digging, so I just said goodnight and went back to bed. Once again, anything for an easy life.

Just down the road from me was a Nigerian bakery that was owned by a friendly guy who I got on well with. I could smell his bread from halfway along the road. I couldn't see how anyone could resist going in there for bread or some pies or cakes. We always had a good chat too. It was nice to catch up with all the goings-on and get the latest news. I always entered his shop with a smile, which he usually reciprocated.

"Morning, Tinuke," he said, sounding both serious and embarrassed. That was the first time I hadn't been greeted with a smile.

"Good morning," I said, confused.

"How's Femi these days? Is he keeping busy?"

"Oh, yeah. He's always out working. I hardly ever see him." I gave a short laugh.

"Well, I'm sorry to tell you this, but... it seems he hasn't been entirely honest with you."

Although this was news to me, it didn't come as any great surprise. I had to try to pretend to be shocked though, just to save face. "What? Why? What do you know?"

I went out last night to a club. You know Peers One?"

While I'd never been to Peers One myself, I had heard of its notoriety. "Yes, I have heard of it. Why?"

"He was there, drunk, making a fool of himself with the young girls."

"What? Flirting?"

The baker nodded. "Tinuke, if I were a betting man, I'd bet that... Well, you know?"

"Yeah, I know what you're trying to say. Thanks for telling me."

"No problem. Enjoy your bread."

"Thanks, I will." Truth be told, I had gone right off it.

Next time I went out, I bumped into an old friend called Boye, who told me he had seen Femi there too. He was definitely up to something.

As always, I didn't want to upset the applecart, so I just let this go. It was summer time, and we were enjoying days out as a family. On one occasion, we had a really nice time, and everyone was happy. I took the children back inside, expecting him to follow, but there was no sign.

When the children gave me a moment of peace, I heard voices. At first I thought it was someone outside with their phone on hands-free. But no, it was Femi. I put the air pods in my ears.

From then on I never saw him. This was especially noticeable at weekends, when we were meant to have spare time. It was just one excuse after another. By this time I was certain he was up to his old tricks, but I couldn't help questioning myself, wondering if it was just me imagining things again.

So I had an idea. If he was too busy to spend any time with *us*, maybe we could spend time with *him*. So, with this in mind, I suggested that we go with him on a delivery one day.

About an hour into the journey the phone rang.

"Hi, how's it going?" He started laughing and whoever it was laughed too, even though he hadn't said anything remotely funny.

The laughing and joking continued for five minutes or so, until he said with an air of caution in his voice, "Err… I'll say hello to Tinuke, shall I?"

There was no doubt in my mind that this was to inform whoever it was that I was in the car. Their tone changed immediately, and he said goodbye. From the way he looked at me and then scowled through the windscreen without saying a word, I could tell he was angry with me for being there.

Not more than ten minutes after he clattered his phone onto the dashboard, she called again. She asked him where he was, so he told her not far. Just before they hung up, she asked if he could drop something off.

It was obvious from the moment we pulled up that he felt awkward. However, I was having none of it. "Femi, wait for me," I called, getting out of the truck.

He looked at me with an expression that was a combination of annoyance, embarrassment and guilt, if such an expression exists.

She was there waiting at the door, all smiles, clearly delighted to see him. I took a closer look and realised that I knew her. She was a friend of my cousin's, who had only recently turned 21. He said something inaudible to her under his breath and gestured for us to follow.

After a short, mumbled conversation, she looked at me over his shoulder and smiled. "Come in, take a seat, how are you, do you want a drink?" I didn't say much in reply, but did my best to remain polite at all times. Then she sat down on the couch and started talking to me about what I did and my life at home with the kids. She was so patronising I could have swung for her.

Thankfully, we weren't in her house very long. I walked back to the truck with my head held high. Neither of us said a word until we turned the corner of her street. "She seems friendly," I said, staring straight ahead.

He clearly didn't know what to say. He kept opening his mouth to say something and then thought better of it.

"Look, whatever it is you're up to with that... girl... I know about it."

"What are you talking about? Oh, dear. There you go again, twisting things round in your head."

"I know about it. Just put a stop to it, OK?"

He shook his head in disbelief. "We're just friends. I'm not going to stop anything."

He always was a master at convincing people he was telling the truth. There was always the possibility that I had got things wrong, so just to keep the peace, I let it drop.

My brother, however, had other ideas.

"Hi," my brother said, stepping in through the front door. "How are you both?"

We got the niceties out of the way, and then, once we were all settled in the living room, my brother got serious.

"I have something to tell you. To you, Tinuke."

If I was curious, Femi looked nonplussed.

"It's Femi. He's been going behind your back."

I don't know what compelled me to fake surprise. "What? With who?"

My brother waved away Femi's protestations and spilt the beans.

Turned out he'd been messing around with that friend of my cousin's. He had gone to deliver something once and then he'd been making up reasons to go there all the time. This had been compounded when he failed to make a collection.

"No, you've got it wrong. We're best mates. Nothing else." He sounded so pathetic.

My brother was having none of it. "Oh, don't give me that. What's with your track record?"

A huge argument ensued, which ended up with Femi admitting his guilt.

I sat in silence, waiting for my brother to drive off while I gave the matter some thought. "I've had enough."

"What do you mean, you've had enough?"

"I want you to leave, that's what I mean."

"Fine." He packed his bags and stormed out.

That wasn't the end of it. From that moment on, everyone kept coming around, telling me what I should and shouldn't be doing. They told me to forgive him and take him back, but this time I stood firm. I was determined to change my ways.

A week or two later, I got word that Femi had gone to live with his friend in Crawley. He carried on working for my brother, all the while pestering me to take him back.

"No," I said, "you've done what you wanted to do. Just move on with your life. We're OK." He did as I asked, but never once sent money to help pay for his children's upbringing. For the first time I understood that if we broke up, I was going to struggle to pay for childcare costs by myself.

I felt very alone because it was just me against a whole nation who sees violence as a part of Nigerian culture. The very person who was assigned to be a protector for me and my children was in fact abusing us. And he was backed by all. It's safe to say that narcissism is also a part of the Nigerian culture: poor interpersonal relationships between spouses, friends and family.

Family… That's just a word that means nothing. The family dynamics generally are very unhealthy, manipulative and controlling, and it took all of this to happen to me to realise mine wasn't as westernised as I'd like to think.

No wonder there is a lot of suppressed anger, because people are not allowed to freely express themselves and go towards things that truly make them happy.

I thought about this long and hard and decided I don't belong to this tribe. So if I wasn't going to spend the rest of my life in solitude, I'd have to find a tribe of my own.

If I was going to struggle, I'd rather do it without the interference of everyone around me, so I decided to follow my own advice and move away to an entirely new location. My sister had moved to Nottingham, so that seemed like as good a place as any. I visited her a few times, and we really liked it, so I popped into an estate agent to make a few viewing appointments.

Immediately, I found the perfect house, and I began the application process. The only problem was, my bank account was almost empty. I had all the money for the deposit and estate agent's fee and everything else you needed to pay when you're buying a house, so that went through without a hitch. When it came to the solicitors fees, however, I came up short. Unless I found the money soon, I'd be stranded.

Sometime before, I had lent money to some of his friends. They were doing well by this time, so he told me, so I thought now might be a good time to ask for it back. It had always felt awkward before, and it still did, but desperate times call for desperate measures. It was only £2,000, but at least it was a foundation to build on.

I went round there with high hopes, but they were soon dashed. They went quiet and then invited me inside. "Why do you need it now, just when we're getting back on our feet?" They were obviously shocked at my inability to muster up what they considered to be a small amount of money.

"I wouldn't ask, honestly, but it's urgent."

"Urgent? Why?"

I explained that I needed my money to buy a property in Nottingham, so that I could start a new life among friends. "Femi isn't supporting me at all. I have two children to bring up on my own. I have a full-time job, and I'm broke."

They had their own private conversation for a minute before replying. "I'm sorry, Tinuke. We'd love to help, but we can't go behind Femi's back. Sorry."

"What? Why can't you? I lent you the money in good faith, and I need it back. It has nothing to do with him."

"Sorry."

I had two children to look after, no money and nowhere to live. Things soon took a turn for the worse.

"Hi, babe,"

He walked in as if nothing had happened.

"What are you doing here?"

"I heard from my friends that you have bought a house. Is it true?"

"No. I need money for the deposit. And they wouldn't—"

"I'll see what I can do. Let me talk to them, OK?"

I didn't want to accept his offer of help, but I had no choice. "OK, thanks." I knew that somewhere along the line, he'd make me regret this.

To my surprise, he came back the next day, with £1,200. "Here," he said, handing over the money. "To pay your solicitor's fees."

"Thanks." I knew that somewhere along the line he was going to make me regret this.

"So, when do I get to see it?"

Chapter Nine
Did I make the right choices for me?

The woman at the estate agent told me to sit on a plush green chair and went into a back room to fetch the paperwork. As soon as she disappeared, the sounds of the street outside filtered in, and a woman wearing dark glasses sat at a table across the aisle. The sight of her brought everything flooding back.

On reflection, I realised that I was never ready to get married, nor did I want to. I just wanted to fit in so that all the gossiping and talking behind my back would stop. I was so desperate to be accepted that I let myself fall for the first halfwit that came along. I guess all I wanted was to be held in the same esteem as my sister and friends.

So I started to think about where it had gone wrong and if it could be pinpointed to a specific moment or wrong decision.

I'm not sure how the thought first popped into my head, but when I went back to work after Funmi, the time felt right to start planning our engagement party. I felt really positive at that time, with sky-high confidence, so maybe I got a bit carried away with myself. We were going to have a grand day, with relatives from here, there and everywhere. I was going to wear a nice dress, the kind I used to when we first met, and he was going to look handsome in his new gear too.

It was September 2015. I greeted him with a smile, in response to which he grunted and turned his back on me, but that was nothing unusual. "Honey," I shouted, following him into his room.

"Yes?"

"Don't you think it's time we started planning our engagement party?"

"Yeah, OK."

I wasn't naïve enough to take this as read, but I wasn't going to complain.

"I've got a few ideas."

He sat next to me on the couch, and we spent an hour or so visiting various websites, trying to find the perfect venue and comparing prices.

We didn't decide there and then; of course not. We strung it out as long as possible because it was a process we both enjoyed. We drew up a shortlist, and then he informed me of his choice. I have to admit that it did look appealing, so I went along with it. As soon as he left the room, I looked at the prices and discovered that this was the most expensive option by a distance. It was going to cost us £15,000.

"Have you seen the price?"

He nodded. "Come on, it's not all that much, is it?"

He was obviously expecting me to pay. "I suppose not."

"Come on, don't be like that. I'll go halves with you, OK?"

"Oh, yes. Thanks, hun. I can't wait. Can you?"

We booked the party for the following month and then made our way to the bedroom.

On the eve of the party, everything seemed to be running like clockwork. In the morning, he went to collect his mum, who had come all the way from Nigeria. At first glance, she was a warm, amicable person, whom I felt I could trust. She hugged me, kissed me on the cheek and then asked where the kettle was. It was nice to have someone make me a cup of tea, which endeared me to her right away.

We spent an hour or so chatting. I enjoyed hearing stories of his childhood. However, she wouldn't hear a single word said against her precious son. Not even when it was said in jest.

Everything was still going great guns the next morning. I had been up a long while, making preparations, and I was on the couch chatting to his mum when he emerged from his room. Someone knocked.

"One minute," he called, grinning, rushing to the door. I couldn't see who it was, but there was a lot of back-slapping going on. They had Irish accents. He had been telling me about his friends in Dublin for some time and had insisted they come to the party. I agreed to this, despite my reservations.

"I'm just going out for a while," he shouted over his shoulder. "My friends here have no place to stay."

"Fine. How long will you be?"

He sighed and muttered something under his breath. Once the laughing and whispering had run its course, he called, "About an hour."

Yeah, right.

Come 5 pm, and I was sat on the couch, talking to his mum through a wall of awkwardness. I could tell that, just like me, she was feeling uneasy about her son's disappearing act.

"It's not the first time he's done this, I—"

She waved a hand. "Shhh. He's never done this before in my life. He's usually very punctual."

I didn't want us to start bickering over a chance remark. "I'll call him."

I let it ring for almost a minute before I hung up. The same thing happened ten minutes later, and ten minutes after that. I left it another half an hour before I tried again, but there was still no reply.

The kids had gone to bed, and we really started to panic. His mum just sat there staring into space, ordering me to call him again and again. Her eyes were bloodshot, and she staggered when she got up to visit the bathroom, but she was too worried to sleep.

I didn't have his mother's delusions, but I was worried nonetheless. All sorts of things kept running through my mind. What if he was lying dead in a ditch somewhere? I rang my tongue around my mouth to generate some saliva as I held the phone to my ear.

The kids were up, and we were enjoying a cup of tea when the front door banged shut and footsteps approached. I smiled at his mum, who put her hand over her heart and mouthed, "Thank God."

We both ran to greet him. He hugged his mother and smiled at me before muttering some kind of lame excuse. His breath stank of alcohol. He staggered into the living room with his mum and the kids while I cooked him some breakfast.

"Thanks for that; it was really nice," he said, scraping his plate with the edge of his fork.

"Thanks." He was in a good mood. I might just get away with it. "So what happened? Why did you come home late?"

He smiled and shook his head angrily. "I was waiting for that. Always so many questions. What the hell's wrong with you? Tell her, Mum."

"He's right. He needs to have some freedom. Just lay off him."

"No. We had a pre-engagement party last night. You didn't show up. That's NOT acceptable. We were trying to call you all night. Why did you switch your phone off?"

His eyes glazed over. "You always have to start something, don't you?"

"You—"

It happened so quick that I didn't even see it coming. I screamed out as my hand shot up to my face. I was determined not to cry, even though I wanted to. He struck me again, the opposite cheek this time, and once more. Sat with my face in my hands, his hot breath on the back of my neck, I knew his mum was going to take his side.

"It's off," I declared, looking up, blood and tears dripping onto my blouse.

He looked at his mother and shrugged.

Ten minutes later I was on my own with our kids.

"Mum," I said, pressing the phone to my ear.

"What? Did he come back?"

I told her everything, from how I'd spent the night worrying myself sick, to the moment he'd stormed out. My mum informed me that she was coming over right away.

It wasn't just her who came though. When she arrived, she was with the entire family.

My brother ran in and put his arm around my shoulder. By the time I turned around, I felt I was on trial.

"What do you mean, you called it off?" My mum said disapprovingly.

"I couldn't go through with it, could I?" I pointed to my face. "Look. Am I meant to put up with this? You're telling me this is OK?"

My mum sighed and turned to face my grandma. "You talk to her, will you?"

My grandma placed her hands on her lap and leant in. "Did I tell you about your grandpa?"

I didn't know how to answer this question, so I just said the first thing that came into my head. "No."

"He had nine wives. That's what things were like back then. But now—you don't know how easy you got it. Just be happy with your lot, will you?"

I threw an incredulous glance at my sister, who just nodded as if to say my grandma was right.

The front door banged shut. Footsteps approached.

"What the—"

His mum stormed towards my mum. "Have you seen this situation? Have you seen what your daughter's done now?"

"My daughter? He hit her. Look at her face." My mum always stuck up for me to other people.

"Did she tell you Femi did that? Is that what she said?"

My mother nodded sheepishly.

"She was lying. What's wrong with her? The lies constantly drip off her tongue."

It was time for me to speak up. "I'm not lying."

"So it looks like you can't even tell the truth now. In front of all these people." She faced my mum. "Your daughter's gone and ruined my sons' life. He was doing just fine until he met her."

My mum was torn between her loyalty to me and her reluctance to go against the grain. It was like they were all scared about what everyone else thought.

So that was it. The only person who wanted to have anything to do with me was my brother.

This happened two years ago.

The estate agent returned. "Sorry about that."

I jumped. "Oh, I was miles away."

She pushed the documents across the desk for me to go through one final time before I signed on the dotted line.

I arrived home to find he had finished his morning deliveries. "Hi, babe. How did it go?"

"It went well. I paid up and signed." I had a moment of weakness. "I'm gonna miss you," I said, getting all teary-eyed.

"What? What do you mean you're gonna miss me? I'm coming too, right? We're a family, right?"

"Yes, but… It was meant to be a fresh start. Come on, things haven't been working out between us, have they?"

His phone rang. I could tell right away that it was his mother.

"She's doing fine. Oh, I have some great news, Mum. We've bought a house. Yeah, we're moving to Nottingham!"

I instinctively reached across to try to grab the phone. "No, we didn't decide that."

He waved me away and started talking to her about something else.

"That was my mum," he said, grinning as he shoved his phone back in his pocket.

"I gathered as much."

"She's really happy for us. She said to pass on her congratulations."

"We didn't agree that you were coming with me. I thought—"

"Yeah, but you didn't mean that, did you? We're a family, right? I know things haven't been going smoothly lately, but a fresh start will do us good. Come on, I'm sorry. From now on, I'm a changed person."

He was living in a one-bedroomed flat at the time. It was part of a shared house in London. It was obvious to anyone with half a brain why he wanted to come with me—and it had nothing to do with us being a family or his remorse. No, it was all about his image. It didn't look good him being in a one-bedroomed flat, so he wanted to come so he could say he was a family man with his own house. That would earn him some respect.

"Well, what do you say?"

I put everything to the back of my mind and gave it a moment's thought. If I moved alone, I'd have to face the consequences from my family. I'd also have to explain to the community in Nottingham why I was single and have them ostracise me, or worse still, try to pair me off with someone. I might be just as unhappy there on my own, and…

"Oh, OK." I'd been putting up with it for this long, so I could continue in Nottingham. It was a worthwhile trade-off.

He smiled and nodded. "Well, we'd best start making some preparations. You just leave everything to me."

Next thing I knew, all my friends and family were on the phone congratulating me for making the right decision. They kept telling me not to worry about a thing, and that God would bless me. I knew they meant well, but it did nothing to endear me to them. Even his mother, whom I'd hardly ever spoken to, got in on the act. I still had doubts about whether I was doing the right thing, but they obviously counted for nothing.

I have to admit that Femi was a great help with the move—and, yes, he did take care of everything. In all the time I'd known him, that must have been the only time he kept a promise.

My brother agreed to stay in the flat in London, which meant we could move bit by bit. The only day that really sticks out in my memory was the day Femi and I clapped eyes on our new house.

"You have to be kidding me," he said as we pulled up outside the terraced house.

"I know it's not much—"

"Damn right, it's not. Who in their right mind would live in a place like this? Who did you buy it from?"

"An old lady," I mumbled.

He nodded. "Makes sense. What the hell possessed you? And you expected me to move in with you? Next time you consult me *before* you go making any rash decisions about my future, OK?"

I wanted to remind him that I'd only involved him because I was flat broke, and it wasn't meant to be about *his* future, but I just couldn't be bothered with all the bickering. "OK," I said. This was one promise I had no intention of keeping.

I carried out a thorough inspection while he sat on the couch and sulked like a child. I already knew there was a lot of renovating to do, but once done, it would make a sound investment. I could sell in a couple of years with a nice tidy profit and then move on to bigger and better things.

I made a note of what needed to be done in each room. More or less the entire house needed a lick of paint, and some rooms needed wallpapering too. There wasn't any structural damage or damp or anything like that. There was no reason at all to suppose that it wouldn't be a safe environment to bring children up in.

Having completed my inspection, I sat down beside Femi and tried to picture what it might be like if the fresh start did us good. We'd have money, he'd be away from his bad influences and I'd have a network of friends. Maybe it had worked out for the best after all. There was also something else, a more practical reason why I had to take him back. For the first time in a very long time I was broke, meaning I was now relying on him to put food on the table while I was off work. It wasn't like before when I just handed him my card. While the likelihood of him stepping up to the plate was slim, I decided to put my faith in him as I had when we first met. I glanced at him, told myself he was a new man and convinced myself that everything was going to be rosy. More fool me.

Chapter Ten
Even Family?

"What you got there?"

I passed him the notes I'd made about the renovations. He shook his head and tutted like a schoolteacher marking a particularly bad exam paper. "Are you mad or what, woman? You drag me all the way here to this old people's house, and now you expect me to do all this bullshit?"

"I'm not expecting you to do anything. I'll do it all myself."

"What, and trust you, like I did with choosing a house? No way."

"Does that mean you're going to do it then?"

He got to his feet and carried out his own inspection.

I soon got tired of listening to him mumbling to himself about me, so I called my sister and invited her over for a coffee and a chat.

I knew that if I went round each room making a start on the decorating work, I'd end up doing and paying for everything myself. So I didn't touch a thing; I just left it for him to do. To his credit, in the end he did this, and I was grateful to my brother for chipping in with the costs. As soon as they had all the necessary materials, they made a start.

I was astonished at his enthusiasm. Each day he'd be hard at it, stripping the walls, sanding things down, pasting the paper. He even pointed out when something needed another coat of paint and did this also. My brother helped a lot too. From what I could see, they were both enjoying the process, which, in turn, made me happy.

It started to feel like he was a completely different person. I'm not sure how I felt about this though. On the one hand, it meant that we had a chance of a happy life, and on the other, it suggested that I'd been wrong and everyone else had been right about him. I decided to concentrate on the positives.

Things became so good that we started to go out on dates again. My sister looked after the kids, meaning we could spend quality time together, for the first time in what seemed like years. This must have been what was missing in our relationship. I started looking back, thinking about how it all went wrong and convinced myself that it was down to us not seeing enough of each other.

We were all out together as a family: me, Femi, our kids and my sister's lot. We were all laughing, but were tired by the time she left in the early evening. Then the phone rang.

It was my friend, who I hadn't seen for a long while. I'd first met her at a salon when she'd done my hair a few times. We got talking and found we had a lot in common, so we kept in touch. We knew all about each other's relationships, and she seemed to have a good one. A really healthy marriage that showed no signs of being strained at all.

The moment I heard her speak, I knew something was wrong. It turned out that her relationship wasn't so great after all; in fact, it was just as bad as mine had been when we'd lived in London. He had been cheating on her, hitting her, trying to convince her it was all in her mind. To cut a long story short, she sounded like a bit of a wreck, which made me wonder if that was how I came across to people. So I did what any decent friend would do and invited her around to stay at ours while she sorted things out.

We sat down, all three of us, and talked it out. Femi was a great help, offering suggestions and even showing some sympathy, which I didn't think he had in him. It was he who suggested that she move away from her husband and make a fresh start, as we had. She gave it some thought and then decided it was a good idea. So the next day we went with her to look at a few places.

Maybe it was because she felt pressured, but she decided on the second house we viewed. On the way back, everyone was chattering excitedly. We were both happy for her, and she was relieved to be getting away from her husband. When Femi offered to help her move, she was over the moon. *I'll believe that when I see it.*

It was around that time that I began to notice a change in their relationship. Before, they did get on well, but only when I was there. It was like they could only communicate through me, but now the dynamic had changed, and they were friends in their own right. Often I'd walk into the room carrying a tray of drinks to find them talking and laughing like a couple of old friends. I must admit to feeling a tiny bit suspicious, but I didn't want to judge him by past experiences. Things had been different since we moved, so maybe he had changed. I decided to push my concerns to the back of my mind and focus on the positives, of which there were many.

We all had a great Christmas that year, the best I can remember. There were the two of us, the kids, my sister's lot, my friend, plus everyone else I knew in the area. At this point I was thinking back to how close I was to walking out on all this and moving alone to bring up the children without their father.

The year 2018 was ushered in on a wave of positivity. Femi was always around my friend's house, helping her prepare for the move and even doing one or two spots of decorating. This was a side to him I'd never seen before. And I wasn't the only one who noticed. Suddenly, his friends were envious of his family and beautiful wife with her good job. Then one morning, I felt something move in my stomach, and it was like the whole world collapsed around me.

I didn't want anyone to know, not even the friend who was staying with us, so I waited until they were out before going to the chemist to get a test. Not even an hour after I'd said goodbye to the pharmacist, I was sat on the couch with my head in my hands. What felt like a million thoughts ran round in my head, causing a knot like tangled-up spaghetti. How would it affect our relationship? Would the abuse start again? Would I be able to get more time off work? Would I be sick again? Did I want another child?

I spent the rest of the day trying to answer some of these questions, until Femi and my friend walked in, laughing and joking like best mates. "What's up with you? Why the long face?"

Femi walked towards me with the kind of patronising expression that said I ought to lighten up. I couldn't think of anything to say, so I just shrugged and put on a smile.

Pregnancy tests can be unreliable, so I didn't say anything straight away. I wanted to make absolutely certain before I went spoiling things again, so I let it hang over me for the next week until I could get an appointment at the doctor's, during which time we went here, there and everywhere with my sister and her family.

The doctor confirmed what I already knew. When they came in laughing and joking, wanting to go out somewhere, I lost my courage. I continued to procrastinate until a couple of days later when my friend had gone to visit her family and we were sat on our own. I looked at him, and he turned around so that our eyes locked. He had a glint in his eye that I hadn't seen before. This was the man I fell in love with. This was the person I'd been searching for since I first met him. This was the man for me. It's safe to say that I'd never felt more in love with anyone than I did at that moment. The pregnancy was there at the back of my mind, hanging over me, so I just wanted it out of the way, and if the glint in his eyes remained, then I'd be the happiest woman in the world.

The glint vanished. We sat on opposite sides of the couch for the next couple of hours, separated by a wall of awkwardness as we each tried to work out what the other was thinking. When my friend came in, he jumped to his feet and said we had something to celebrate. My friend kissed me on the cheek and made a right fuss as Femi went out to get a bottle of bubbly.

They both kept going on about how pleased they were for the rest of the night, saying what a great mother I was and all-round terrific woman for juggling a full-time job with looking after the children. The way they were both so incessantly nice to me made me feel a bit uneasy, but I just kept on saying thanks and throwing the odd compliment back in return.

We put a film on, which I pretended to watch while they sat riveted. "Femi, can I have a word?" My friend, discreet as always, left the room.

"I'm having a termination."

The next thing I knew, my mum, sisters, and the entire community were telling me I was about to commit a mortal sin, calling me a murderer, etc. I went to see the pastor who, as you can imagine, was the most vociferous of the lot. It felt like my private affairs were nothing more than a juicy piece of gossip.

My sister, Ayo, came round on a daily basis, trying to talk me out of it. Femi showed some sympathy, so when I went into town one Saturday, I decided to buy him something nice. I said I'd be back in about two hours.

I fully intended to make an afternoon of it, but the weather turned, and I developed this thumping headache. So I bought him a shirt and went back home. The kids were tired, wet and hungry, but I was looking forward to a coffee and a rest after they'd been seen to.

"Hi," I called, stepping in through the doorway. No reply. "Shhh."

The kids did as I asked. There were voices... upstairs... a man and a woman... Femi and my friend.

I grinned and wondered what they could be doing. Quiet as a mouse, I took the kids' coats off and crept up the stairs. The noises got louder with each step I took until—Oh no. Not with my friend, not in my house, not when I'd let myself be sucked in.

Turned out he'd been sleeping with her for some time. Each time he was going around to her house to help with her move, when I'd be at home thinking about how wonderful he was, he was in fact in bed with her.

I couldn't look at either of them, nor any of my family. I didn't want them to tell me it was God's way of punishing me for the abortion.

I was alone with two children, expecting a third, but people just withdrew their support. What surprised me the most was the reaction of my own family. Growing up, I never once thought that they'd just abandon me like they did. You sometimes hear of people saying their son or daughter is dead. That's exactly how it felt

Chapter Eleven
Pain Changed Me

I wanted to burst in, to scream and shout at them, to demand answers, but with my hand on the door handle, I lost interest. This was because I knew the drill. Neither of them was going to show any remorse. Femi was going to make out it was all my fault, and then they were going to carry on with what they were doing. So, in the end, I just went back downstairs and spent some time with the kids.

As young as she was, Funmi could tell something was wrong right away. She sat next to me on the couch, put her head on my shoulder and asked why I was upset. I knew she meant well, bless her, but that set me off crying until I stood up, dusted myself down and marched up the stairs.

"What the—" Femi sat up and smiled at me awkwardly, like I had just caught him wrapping up my Christmas present. At least my so-called 'friend' looked somewhat guilty, but not as guilty as you might expect. It was evident right away that he had got to her. He probably told her how I neglected him, let myself go and went sleeping around behind his back.

"I was just—"

"I know what you were doing, Femi."

When my 'friend' rolled over to put a foot on the floor, he tugged on her sleeve and told her it was OK. I could tell she didn't want to get back into bed with him, but she did as he asked, nonetheless. It was like all his lies had cast a spell on her. I'd lost her for good.

Without saying another word, I closed the door and went back downstairs to look after my children. I switched the TV on so I wouldn't have to sit in my own house and listen to my husband having sex with my friend, but as soon as I had done so, I heard shouting. The door slammed, and she ran down the stairs without looking at me once.

Almost immediately, the ceiling thudded, and he got out of bed, cursing, mumbling about what he was going to do to me. This wasn't an irregular occurrence, so I just carried on playing with the kids.

"Give me the papers for my passport and fuck off out of my life."

I stood firm. "You must be joking."

"Don't defy me, you bitch; you're my wife. You made an oath, remember?"

"I haven't been your wife for a long time. It's over; can't you see?"

"Give me the fucking papers or else—"

"Come on!" I grabbed hold of the kids, ran into the kitchen and slumped down with my back against the door.

Bang, bang, bang. He pounded against the door with his fist. "Come out of there! If I have to come in there and get you, you fuckin' ugly bitch, I'll—"

"You'll what?"

"Right, you just wait." He kicked the door, each blow inching me away from the door.

In the end, it was the sight of my kids sat on the kitchen table, sobbing into their hands, that prompted me to do what I did.

Two minutes later I put my phone back into my pocket and wedged the table between myself and the wall. If I could only keep my legs straight, it might buy us some time.

Just as I was about to buckle under his force, the front door banged. "Open up!"

"Fuck off!" Femi shouted at the top of his voice.

"OPEN UP!"

He stormed off towards the door. "Who the f—"

"Good afternoon, sir. We've received a complaint from this address."

He thumped on the kitchen door. "Did you call the police, bitch? Just wait 'til I—" He never could control his temper.

"Stand aside, sir."

"You must be fuckin' jokin'."

There was another voice, much deeper. I formed a picture of a massive guy in my mind's eye, with his hand on Femi's shoulder. He moved aside, mumbling to himself as he did so.

"So let me get this right; you're threatening the victim, are you?"

"No."

"Glad to hear it."

"Tinuke? Come on, it's the police. Let me in, will you?"

I moved away from the door.

"What the—what's been going on? You shouldn't be sat hiding on the kitchen floor in your condition."

Femi was talking to someone on the phone, telling whoever it was that I'd called the police. From his tone of voice, I could tell that whoever he was talking to was being wholly absorbed by his lies.

"Who's he talking to?" I said to myself, under my breath.

The policeman shrugged and took a peek around the door. "He's hung up now."

About five minutes later the front door opened. I knew from the way she spoke to Femi that it was my sister. I smiled, safe in the knowledge that she was going to put two and two together and come rushing to my aid. "Let me talk to her," I said to the policeman, who stood aside and held the door open for me.

"Get out. I never want to see you again," I yelled at him.

My sister looked at me, inquisitively. "Tinuke, why are you saying this?"

"Because—"

Femi shook his head. "No, I'm not going anywhere. This is my house. This is my family."

"Sir, just pack a bag and leave. Please do as we ask."

"I'm not going anywhere, I told you."

"Sir, you're not acting right towards your wife. We're not going to expose her to any more abuse, so if you don't pack your bags and leave now, we'll have to make you do it by force."

The room filled with a disbelieving silence until the sound of her car faded away into the distance. Then the policeman with the deep, booming voice turned to me and said, "Did you say that was your sister?"

I nodded.

He shook his head in disbelief. "Well, if that's your sister and she's done that, then just you be careful. I would think long and hard before I let those two back into my life."

"Yeah, I know."

After they had taken a statement, the policeman glanced around the room, at my kids and then back at me. "You know I'll have to get social services involved, don't you?"

It was like I had been shot by a poisoned arrow. "What? No, it's not my fault. It's—"

"Relax. No one's going to take your kids away from you, I promise. You're a great mother. Anyone can see that. It's just that, well, it isn't really safe for them to be here with their father likely to come round at any minute, is it?"

"No."

When they left, I sat down, and the reality of the situation hit me. In the space of a few hours, I'd lost a close friend, my husband and my sister. All I had left were my kids. I patted the seat next to me.

It took some getting over, but things were starting to get back to normal a few days later. I was spending some quality time with the kids, taking them to the park and all that, so I was beginning to think that I didn't need him and he had done me a favour by acting the way he had. Then my sister showed up, looking as guilty as sin.

"Good to see you," I said, putting a couple of drinks down on the table. It was the truth too; I was glad to see her, but it was like there was an invisible barrier between us, one that was going to take a pickaxe and a day of hard labour to get through.

"So, how did you know I needed your help?" I said this through gritted teeth, just to break the ice.

"Femi called me and said something was wrong, so I came right over."

"And you took him away with you in your car?"

"Yeah, I needed to make sure you were safe."

"Thanks." I hadn't thought of it that way. Perhaps she was telling the truth, and I'd been blaming her for no reason. "I haven't seen him since."

She shrugged and took a sip of coffee.

"What? Do you know something? Have you seen him?"

"Tinuke, I—"

"What?"

"Femi. He's... he's staying with me."

At one time this would have cut through me like scissors to paper, but I was hardened to it. "Thank you."

"*Thank you?* What for?"

"For taking him in, making sure he was OK."

She smiled and patted my thigh. "That's the spirit. You'll come through this; I promise. I'll call mom, the pastor, all the community, and we'll get it sorted out. We'll have the old Tinuke back in no time."

I opened my mouth to ask how she was finding the sex, but managed to stop myself at the last minute. We sat in silence until she put her empty mug down on the table and left.

Next thing I knew, my mum was on the phone. "Tinuke, why didn't you tell me any of this? Why didn't you confide in your brothers or sisters? That's what families are for, isn't it? We stick together in times of need."

Only the consequences of being disrespectful stopped me from laughing out loud. "I tried, but they're just not interested. They're siding with Femi. Mum, I feel so lonely and isolated. I don't know what to do." I started to cry.

"Tinuke, can't you see that they're siding with Femi because they didn't know?"

"No, Mum, no. Something's happening that's not right, and in time we'll find out."

My mum sighed. "No, Tinuke, nothing's happening. It's all in your mind."

I couldn't take this any more, so I finally snapped. "So, what? You're not going to support me? I'm on my own with two toddlers, I've just caught my husband in bed with my friend, who I took in in good faith, and now he's shacked up with my sister, and you're saying it's all my fault?"

"Shacked up? What are you trying to say, Tinuke?"

"You work it out for yourself."

So that was it, my mum never spoke to me again all the time I was in Nottingham. She must have phoned each of my siblings too, because they offered me no support either. In fact, they were all on his side and outraged at my insinuation. Then things took a turn for the worse.

It started a couple of days later, when I had just got back from the shops and was seeing to the kids. My phone beeped, informing me I had a text message. It was him.

I put the phone back in my pocket and carried on with life as if he didn't exist. Something I should have done long before. My phone kept on beeping all afternoon, until I couldn't bury my head in the sand any longer. I knew I had to read them sooner or later. I waited until the kids had gone to bed, so they wouldn't see me upset and crying again.

I skipped through the first few, as there was nothing new there, just insults, calling me a bad mother etc., which I just shrugged off. Then, after I had counted ten already, there was a message that I couldn't really ignore. Apparently, one of my so-called 'friends', Anu, had gone behind my back and told him she babysat once while I went off to a hotel with my lover. It then transpired that she said I dated men for money, adding that he was better off without me.

I was constantly checking if the doors were locked and living in fear, waiting for his car to thud at any second.

When they phoned, social services asked me all sorts of questions, trying to decide whether I was a fit mother or not. Well, that's how it seemed to start with at least. In the end, they turned out to be quite helpful and even arranged for us to talk through a mediator.

After the first session, which to be honest didn't go all that well, they phoned again to ask if there had been any domestic abuse. When I said there had, she said they were unable to continue with the mediation, but she would get a report done to get some recommendations.

At this point I felt low, as low as I'd ever been. I was abandoned by my husband, my family and now, so it seemed, social services. Things got so bad that I went to see the doctor, who prescribed me some anti-depressants.

I remember sitting at home reading the small print on the back of the box, thinking that if I took them, things might get worse instead of better. I broke down and cried. I prayed to God that he would just take the hurt away and help me cope with everything that was going on in my life.

It was spring, but it could have been midwinter, because I rarely even opened the curtains. I had my kids with me, who still needed caring for. It was them—and only them—who kept me in the land of the living. In a funny sort of way, it pulled us all closer together.

In the night, or when the kids were fast asleep in the morning, I'd stand in front of the mirror and tell myself that I was a mess. I had got back to some semblance of my old self and had then let myself go again. Only this time, I had sunk even deeper down the hole. It was small wonder he'd slept with my friend, because I wasn't attractive. How could I possibly be? I told myself I wasn't even fit to be a mother, and if I had another child, I'd only make its life a misery.

So after a couple of weeks in isolation, I decided to take matters into my own hands and have an abortion. Now I was on my own, I had nothing to fear: no backlash from my family or endless preaching from the pastor. I smiled for the first time since the day it happened. I thought about who there was left to turn to and gave my aunt a call.

"I'm doing OK, but I could do with some support." I made myself vulnerable to her. The last thing I needed now was for her to go the same way as everyone else and tell me I'd got what I deserved for the way I treated Femi. I held my breath as I waited for her to respond.

"But, Tinuke, you're so far away. What are you doing in Nottingham, for heaven's sake?"

She was right. There was no reason for me to be there; none at all. I had gone there for a fresh start, to be near my sister and a few other friends. For a while I'd had it all, but now it had gone. All of it.

"I don't know."

"Are you able to move back here?"

Even though she was right, I was reluctant to admit defeat. "Well, I've only just moved here."

"I can't do anything to help you unless you do."

"OK, I'll see what I can do."

I sat with my chin in my hands for a few minutes, trying to sort things out in my own head before I did anything I might regret.

I had to find somewhere to live that would be suitable for a single mother with two young children. Somewhere not too far out of the way, that would be easily accessible for my aunt, but in an area where I would be safe walking to the shops with my kids. Once I factored in affordability and my commute to work, my options had dwindled down to three. I phoned up right away, only to find that two were no longer available. So I arranged to go and see the only suitable place in the whole of London and prayed that I'd get lucky.

Fortunately, it was reasonable and wasn't all that far to commute. As soon as I got home, I set about putting the wheels in motion. There was a lot to do, much more than before, because now I didn't have anyone to help me. I had to use hired help, which was almost as expensive as the deposit.

Chapter Twelve
Betrayal from Family—
Recovery

A couple of weeks after the move, I was playing a game with the kids when the doorbell rang. It was my aunt, the one who had promised to support me. I led her inside and told her to take a seat.

She got straight to the point. "Tinuke, you misled me, didn't you?"

"What?"

"You misled me. You told me it was Femi who had been abusing *you*, treating *you* badly, sleeping with your friend and terrifying your poor innocent children, when all the time it was—"

"What?"

"When all the time it was *you* doing the cheating. Femi came around, told me how you were promiscuous and a compulsive liar. He said I shouldn't ever believe a word you say, and you know, that got me thinking. Why should I take your word above his? You've been telling lies about him ever since you met him. Why should I believe you? Who in their right mind would?"

Everyone thought I'd gone off and left my husband so I could continue with my promiscuous lifestyle. They all said that the third child, the one I'd aborted, wasn't even his to begin with. They'd been so taken in by his lies that they didn't want to be associated with me. So I had come back to London only to be as isolated as I had been in Nottingham.

I should have known this would happen when my aunt had promised to support me, before I upped sticks and forked out on a move that I couldn't afford. I was tired, not so much of him, but of everyone believing him. I didn't have the strength to be angry, so in the end I just got up and showed her to the door. Looking back, that might have been the wrong course of action, but I was sick of having to prove myself to everyone, just so they'd listen for a minute.

The social services in Nottingham transferred my case to London. Someone came around to give me the results of the report. "If he wants to see the kids, you'll have to go to court."

"I don't want to go to court."

They did their best to get me to change my mind.

I just wanted them to go away and stop bothering me with all their questions. "Is there any other way we can do this, without going to court?"

She gave it a moment's thought. "Well, there is one way. How about he goes to supervised contact, and then after a while, once we're certain it's safe, we could move him to unsupervised."

I needed more information before I could make a decision. "Can you send me a link or something, so I can read up on it?"

"I'm afraid not. If you want to know more, you'll have to do your own research."

I emailed my findings to Femi and asked if he was willing to cooperate. The messages I got in reply can only be described as horrendous. According to him, I was a slut who wanted to stop him seeing his own kids. Something about his tone compelled me to check that the front door was shut, and locked securely.

In the end, I just sent him a link to a supervised contact centre and hoped for the best, but I never got a reply, just a whole load of abuse and accusations.

Every half hour, or so it seemed, my phone beeped. My resolve soon weakened. On the bad days I couldn't bring myself to leave the house or answer the phone to anyone.

When the morning came for me to go back to work, it felt like my old life was back. I took my kids to the crèche, kissed them goodbye and hit the road. By the time I strode into the office, head held high, I felt invincible. I looked around at my colleagues, attempting to communicate that I was back and a force to be reckoned with. It didn't take long for my illusion to be shattered.

As I walked through the office, glad to be back, I saw a couple of my colleagues, one of whom I sometimes saw outside of work. They were sat at my desk, deep in conversation. As I got closer, I picked up snippets of what they were saying.

"We don't really know who's lying. She said *he* abused *her*, and *he* said *she* left because she's a slut, and even her own sister confirmed it."

"It's strange, because she was supporting her sister when she was trying to find her feet after she relocated from Nigeria. They seem to be quite close. The whole thing is weird, but I don't really think she did fraud.

I think the guy is just bitter. She would have been caught by now if she did."

They stopped talking and looked at me, both of them with the same awkward smile that I'd seen on Femi so many times before.

"I believe your husband left you, Tinuke?"

"Well, no, he didn't leave me. I threw him out."

She smirked. "No."

"What do you mean, *no*. What business of yours is it if I—"

"You don't have to explain anything; it's OK."

I smiled. "I know, thanks."

"Femi has already been here and told us everything."

"What did he tell you?"

"Well, about how you've been treating him, going around with men like some kind of promiscuous woman. You threw him out, but only because he found you out and you didn't like it."

"No, that's not what happened."

I'd become the centre of attention. I tried not to get upset, to be the stereotypical strong black woman, but that's just a fallacy. Sat in the Ladies, I dropped my head into my hands and cried.

This hit me far harder than I thought it would. Each day when I woke up, I had to force myself to get out of bed. I got in to work, put on a smile and said hello, like everything was OK. Then I'd hear the gossiping and the laughter behind my back. So I decided to reduce my hours, to help me cope with everything that was going on. My request was turned down.

I struggled on for a while, but it was taking its toll. So, after giving it some thought, I decided to write an email to my contact at Victim Support. The following week, my hours were reduced.

One morning in July, I went to collect Funmi from nursery, to find the manager stood there, waiting for me with her hands on her hips. "We had your ex in here the other day." She said it like she was expecting me to jump for joy.

I reached down and grasped hold of Tomi's hand. "What did he want?"

"For goodness' sake, relax, Tinuke. He just wanted a letter from us."

"What about?"

"Something to say he was a good and active parent. That he had been here to pick up Funmi a few times. That's all." Again, she said it like it was meaningless and I was going to be relieved.

"And you said he was?"

Her eyes widened. "Yes. Did I do something wrong?"

I took hold of Funmi's hand and led both of my kids back to the car.

I called the police right away. They told me to contact my solicitor to see if he could shed any light on it. They did some probing and came back a few days later, saying he needed this to help him get the right to remain in the UK.

And so it continued. All my friends, family and work colleagues were in on it. He told lies to everyone I knew. My kids were all I had. I had been looking forward to going to work for a long time, but now I hated it. I crept in in the morning, trying to remain as inconspicuous as possible, but I could hear them all whispering and laughing as I passed. I sat in a corner of the room, with my back to them all, getting on with my work, trying to make it look like I wasn't affected in the slightest.

One Saturday, when I was on my own, staring at the blank TV screen, my phone kept beeping over and over. I decided that if I was going to be the strong woman I wanted to be, I had no choice but to call the police. They said they were going to try to get me some protection.

The first step in the lead up to the court case was for both of us to be interviewed by the police. The officer who spoke to me was a big guy with dark hair and a moustache, really intimidating. He took me down this long corridor and into an interview room right at the end. I got a sense that it had been used perhaps only a couple of hours before by a policeman who was interrogating a common criminal. From that moment on, I knew what to expect.

He asked me some really difficult questions, making me recount everything over and over—about my infidelity, my anger and my obsession with revenge. When he was finished, he got to his feet and held the door open for me. No goodbye. No thank you. Nothing. I heard him chatting with another police officer, and then they burst out laughing.

That was only the start of it. They called me back time and time again, asking me the same questions. I got the same policeman each time, who looked like some kind of sadist. I never once got word that they interrogated him in the same way.

On the morning of the trial, I went into work as normal and told my boss that I had to leave around 9.45 am to get to the Stratford Magistrate and Family Court, for ten. After a few seconds' awkward silence, she said it was fine. I thanked her and promised I'd be back after lunch.

The minute I reported in, I realised I had got hold of the wrong end of the stick. The clerk took my name and, without looking up, held her pen in the direction of a long corridor. "Last door on the right."

The room was full of other women, sat quietly, looking at the floor, or the walls opposite. A Pakistani woman wearing a headscarf looked up and smiled as I took a seat. We got talking, and it turned out she was in court for the same thing, and that she had also been told 10 am. In fact, everyone in the room had been told 10 am. By the time my case would be heard, it would be mid afternoon at best. My boss wasn't going to be happy.

All of them looked like stereotypical beaten wives wearing worn out, scruffy clothes and weary expressions. I was the only one of them in smart work attire, so everyone who came in assumed I was a solicitor.

Most of the women in the room were of ethnic minorities. We'd all had exactly the same experiences. We had all been abused mentally and physically and then left at his mercy, to threaten us more for going to the police.

There was this really loud white girl there too. She kept talking about her husband, calling him all the names under the sun and saying what she would do if she ever walked into a room and found him asleep, or passed out from drink. She pulled out a picture to show us the bruises from when he'd slapped her. "I was relieved when the police got hold of him and put him in prison."

We all gasped and looked at each other. "What? They put him in prison?" I glanced round at the others, who just shook their heads in disbelief.

"The police have been really good about this. I'm not their biggest fan, but they're great when it comes to things like this, aren't they?"

"Are they?"

"Yeah, really understanding. Made me a cup of tea and everything. I had this really nice WPC who knew exactly how I felt. She could tell how vulnerable I felt. Gave me a massive hug when I started to cry and told me she'd put me in touch with the legal aid guy."

"And did you get it? The legal aid?"

"Yeah? Didn't *you*?"

I took a deep breath and shook my head.

She grinned. "Oh, look at you. You're much stronger than I am. You'll win your case no problem. You don't need a solicitor, do you?" To be fair, she thought she was paying me a compliment.

I looked up at the ceiling and shook my head. The only difference between me and her was the colour of our skin. Now it all made sense.

He didn't even have the decency to show up. They put me in the stand and kept asking me the same questions over and over, making me recall every last detail. When they asked me if we were actually married, I didn't know what to say. I didn't know if I should reveal if he was a bigamist, because that could open a whole new can of worms that might involve a new trial and a fresh pack of lies.

After a short recess, I walked back in with my head held high. He was given a molestation order, making it illegal for him to contact me or any of my family for a year. I smiled throughout my entire journey back to work, but my positivity dissipated when I saw the look on my boss's face and heard all the whispering and laughing.

Only a couple of days after the non-molestation order was given to him, I got a letter from his solicitor. I was going to court again, three months later, in February 2019. This time it was my kids' futures that were on the line.

Chapter Thirteen
Ready

This was all I needed. I'd been waiting for it to arrive, but that didn't soften the blow. I folded the letter, put it back in the envelope and tried to find some positives. It was five months away, not the following week, giving some precious breathing space. My mum suggested I go to Nigeria for a couple of weeks to recharge my batteries.

Ten minutes later I was on the internet looking for flights to Nigeria, and I found one decently priced so i booked immediately. I was expecting a lot of important letters, but my friend would take care of that for me if I gave her a key.

I'll never forget getting off the plane. The feeling of being absorbed in the warm sunshine that I'd forgotten all about. As soon as our eyes locked, my mum ran towards us and scooped the kids up in her arms.

That was a great night, the best of the entire trip. We spent hours catching up, sharing the odd bit of news that we hadn't talked about over the phone. One of my cousins who I hadn't seen in years came round, and she suggested that we meet up the next day to go on a family excursion. I agreed right away, even though I still felt shattered from the flight.

We had such a good time that we did it again, the next day and the next. On the third day, my mum got a bit disgruntled, so I spent the day shopping with her instead. My cousin appeared again when we got home late that night, and we got talking. I told my mum we were going out on our own the next day, and she reluctantly gave us her blessing. She agreed to have the kids and let us go off to spend some quality time on our own.

About an hour into the trip, we had just passed some traffic lights when a lorry cut across us.

We didn't have a prayer.

"We're going to be killed!" My cousin let out a piercing scream as the lorry screeched and swerved.

I woke up to find myself strapped into a bed, unable to move a muscle. A paramedic leant over me and smiled. She was glad I had come around but didn't sound surprised. She said that we would soon be back at the hospital, where I'd be assessed.

They kept me strapped up in a tiny bed for a couple of days. At that point I was just relieved to be in Nigeria and not London, because here I had people I could rely on to take proper care of the kids.

The doctor told me I was lucky my injuries were not life-threatening as he drew the curtains around my hospital bed. He was right.

He told me once again I'd been fortunate, but that it wasn't advisable to travel anywhere for the time being or I might end up in a wheelchair for the rest of my life. I tried protesting, told him all about the court case, but he just waved a hand and said I wasn't going anywhere for twenty-six weeks.

So that was it. I was staying with my family in Nigeria, and the court case would have to be deferred. Again. First thing I did, before I got any nasty letters, was gather all

ENI ALUKO

the evidence and send it over to Stratford Magistrate and Family Court.

When I didn't hear back, I tried to be positive and convinced myself that everything was OK, but deep down I knew this was a bad sign.

My intuition was correct. Just a few days after the hearing was due to take place, my friend called to say I'd had a letter and to prepare myself for the worst. They were making all kinds of threats, asking why I hadn't attended the hearing, as if I was a lowlife who didn't know any better.

I rang the court right away. The woman I spoke to sounded sympathetic and apologised more than once for the misunderstanding.

The letters kept on coming though. I sent the documents over again and again, but each time it was like I hadn't sent anything at all. The clerk kept on saying she was sorry, and as far as she knew, there was no reason why the court case couldn't be deferred to a later date, as I'd sent the proof so many times. The letters continued, each one more irate than the last. They even threatened to seize my assets. It was like I was shouting at a brick wall.

Then one day my friend in London scanned the letter and held it up for me to read. I could tell from the look on her face, before I'd even read a word, that it had finally arrived. The second hearing was to be held at Clerkenwell and Shoreditch County Court and Family Court, in August 2019.

I thanked her, switched off the computer and sat back while I took it all in. When the doctor agreed that I could go home, I felt a mixture of relief and disappointment.

While I arrived back in the height of summer, it felt like the middle of winter compared to Nigeria. But I soon got warm when I stepped on the Underground platform and into the hot, dirty air.

When I'd unpacked, made the kids something to eat and got settled, I looked through the window for a few minutes to catch a glimpse of the world outside. There wasn't much worth coming home for. It took me a good half hour before I plucked up the courage to start on the pile of letters that my friend had bundled together and placed on the coffee table.

I flicked past the ones from the court, but I knew I had to go back to reread them carefully in the light of day.

It didn't make things seem any better. They were still threatening to take away my assets. His solicitor was still trying every which way he could to frighten me so that I'd be afraid to speak up when the day came. Of course, I'd read all this information before, but it didn't stop me thinking things through over and over again, just to see if I had missed a trick and if there was a way I could have stayed in Nigeria.

I only had one day to settle in before I started getting visitors, who, I could tell, meant well. They were all interested to know about my time in Nigeria and asked me about my back. But as soon as the conversation turned towards the court case, I sensed a change in their tone. My sister was the first to contribute.

"Tinuke, why are you doing this? Why are you going to court to stop Femi from seeing his children? He has done nothing wrong. Don't take this the wrong way, but you're coming across like you're a bit... well... obsessed."

After the way she'd betrayed me, nothing really surprised me. In fact, by this time I didn't expect anything else.

So I didn't talk about it again, only to my mum and the people I'd caught up with in Nigeria. Their attitudes were completely different. They supported me through thick and thin and kept on saying that sooner or later he was going to get what he deserved.

Before I knew it, the day arrived. I went to bed early the night before—only about a couple of hours after I'd put the kids to bed—just to make sure I was extra alert and wouldn't forget anything. I knew I had to be on my guard because his solicitor would try every trick in the book to put the blame on me. Well, that was the plan anyway.

I tried closing my eyes, but all I could think about was the next day. For the first time, it really sank in that there was a chance he might win custody, and they'd take the children from me. It was just a tiny chance, but it was a chance nonetheless; and while this possibility loomed, I couldn't see how I'd ever manage to sleep again.

I could feel everyone staring at me quizzically, wondering why I was shaking as I opened the doors to the court and walked over to the reception desk.

The woman behind the desk gestured for a security guard to go rummaging around in my bag to check I wasn't carrying anything dangerous. When he gave me the all-clear, the receptionist pointed along the corridor to a lift that would take me to the sixth floor.

I stepped into the waiting room, which was full of desperate-looking people accompanied by their solicitors. Some of them were chattering away, while others sat looking at the floor in silence. As soon as I had taken my place among them, I knew exactly what they were feeling.

After five minutes of constant fidgeting, shuffling from side to side, trying to get my legs comfortable, I felt the desperate urge to visit the ladies. I had only been back in the waiting room for five minutes when I got the urge again.

Roughly ten minutes before the case was due to start, I was told to leave the main waiting area and go into a smaller side room. The knot in my stomach that had been tightening all morning got to the stage where I'd likely break a nail if I tried to unpick it.

I opened the door, took a step back and blinked. My brother left his seat to greet me and told me everything would be OK. My solicitor nodded and returned to his notes. My ex looked at me like I was an alcohol-induced vomit in the gutter. Looking straight ahead, I walked past him, my breathing becoming increasingly shallow with each step I took.

As soon as I was seated, his solicitor looked up, pushed his glasses up along the bridge of his nose and coughed to get my brother's attention.

"Tell me, why did your sister give my client shelter after he was asked to vacate the premises?"

My brother looked right through me before he replied. "Because he was family. He didn't have anywhere else to go. I would have done the same."

Halfway through the hearing, I decided I had to get away, leave everything behind and start again. I couldn't cope with the constant questions, insinuations and everyone taking his side any more. My mind drifted towards the time I'd spent in Nigeria. I told the judge I wanted to relocate.

Without giving it a second's thought, the judge shook his head. "That is not a matter for this court. If you want to relocate, you will have to apply separately. Furthermore, I am imposing a prohibitive steps order. Under no circumstances must you leave the UK with your children."

That was it. I had to go home and wait for the date of another hearing. I was in precisely the same position I'd been in the day before, but at least I could stop worrying about losing my kids for a while. Later on, after they'd gone to bed, I sat on the couch and replayed the day's events in my mind. I clenched my fists so tight that my nails dug into my palm. I wanted to scream for someone to put an end to everything.

It wasn't too long before I thought about ending it myself. I had almost made up my mind when I looked at my kids and asked myself if, when they got older, would they look back and think I had been selfish? I couldn't leave them, no matter what.

I did think about going to talk to the pastor, but when I saw him on the street, he just ignored me and looked the other way, like I wasn't there.

The pastor wasn't the only one that did this; it was the whole community. Everyone I saw asked me why I was stopping him from seeing the kids. I explained that it wasn't my decision, and it was just the way things were done in England, but they didn't listen.

I stopped going to the RDM Church altogether.

Chapter Fourteen
Recovery

While I had been in Nigeria, I'd panicked about where I was going to live when I got back to England, so my aunt offered me one of her flats.

I was grateful and everything, but it wasn't exactly suitable for a family with two children. It was, infact, a studio flat. When I arrived in August, I fully intended to return to Nigeria a month later, but because of the court order, I couldn't. And of course, with it being a student flat, soon there would be students. I had a month to find somewhere else to live.

The social services in Hammersmith & Fulham, where my aunt lived, weren't much help. They just kept on passing the buck, saying I was someone else's problem, because they couldn't work out what to do with me. To make matters worse, being a property owner meant I ticked all the wrong boxes.

The woman I saw was middle-aged, with glasses perched on the end of her nose. At first glance, she looked approachable enough, but appearances can be deceptive. She just read my case, shook her head and said, "So you are applying for accommodation when you're a homeowner? Is that what you're saying?"

She wouldn't give me a chance to answer. "Yeah, but—"

"I'll have to report this. You are aware that you are technically committing fraud?"

"But—"

She waved a hand. "I'm sorry, there's nothing we can do. If you're as desperate as you claim to be, you'll be able to find somewhere yourself. There are lots of landlords advertising in the newspaper. Goodbye!"

It was all very well for them to dismiss me and tell me to get a place in the private sector, but there was another tiny detail that they'd overlooked, not that it would have mattered to them anyway. I was unemployed. I had no payslips to prove to a private landlord that I was a reliable tenant.

I spent hours trawling the Internet, searching over and over again on every listing's website imaginable. But every time I came across a house that might be suitable, the agency put a block on it the minute they found out I wasn't in full-time employment.

After a couple of weeks with one setback after another, I had no choice but to go back to social services and humiliate myself in front of that witch again. "Oh no," she said, shaking her head. "We can't help you, as previously communicated." She was enjoying it.

I trudged home, trying to put a brave face on for the kids, but I wasn't fooling them. They wondered why I wasn't laughing and talking to them as I normally did, and why I was no fun. I didn't want them to be affected in any way, so I racked my brains, trying to think of where to go next. I hadn't tried the social services in Tower Hamlet yet, where I'd lived before I went to Nottingham.

I spent half the day travelling on the Underground. I wanted to get there bright and early, which meant braving the rush hour. So I spent twenty minutes with my face pressed into the arm of a man who looked like an angry bulldog.

The woman at Tower Hamlet wasn't quite as bad as the woman at Hammersmith & Fulham, but the outcome was the same. She listened, shook her head, called me a fraudster and told me to go back to Hammersmith & Fulham. I had to smile and thank her on my way out, but inside I wanted to do something entirely different.

I was delighted to find out that the woman I had spoken to previously had been moved, and in her place was a man who at least pretended to be interested. I showed him the documents from the court, proving beyond reasonable doubt that I couldn't go back to Nigeria. He scanned over them and passed them back. It wasn't enough.

I'd recently let my house in Nottingham, so I reached into my bag and produced the agreement. I explained that until the tenancy had run its course, I couldn't go back, or else I'd be in breach of contract. He took it from me and started scrutinising the small print like he was some kind of solicitor. I could tell he was going to find something, so I threw in my safeguard for good measure. He gave in.

"There's nothing I can do right now, but I'll look into it. I'll run a check and get back to you."

I reiterated my address, just so he couldn't turn around and say he didn't have it.

That was a Tuesday. I spent the rest of the week searching for a solution, while constantly listening out for my phone. Whenever it rang, I immediately checked the number, but it was all to no avail. By the end of the following week, things had become desperate.

That Friday night, I put the kids to bed as normal and then sat staring at the blank TV screen while the world went by outside. I picked my phone up a couple of times, eager to find a shoulder to lean on, but I knew there was no one. I'd just have to get through on my own, but the trouble was, my reserves of strength had all but run dry.

As soon as my head hit the pillow, I knew it was going to be one of those nights. It being a Friday and all, the world was alive outside, and I could hear litter—discarded by people out on the town—rattling along the pavement. When someone parked their car and started blasting out music, I gave up and put the light back on. I started thinking, and once I did this, there was no way I was ever going to get any sleep.

I staggered out of bed and slumped down on the couch. My eyes stung from tiredness and my head ached from overthinking things. I just needed something to calm my nerves, to stop me churning things over and over. I wished I could live a more carefree life, where my own needs took precedence over everything. I wished I could be more like him. When the smell of cigarettes started to drift in through the open window, I had an idea.

"Hi," I said to one of the people living downstairs, who I've never so much as smiled at before.

He looked at me quizzically. "Hello. He took a long drag of his cigarette. "Fancy a fag?"

I nodded. "Yes, if you wouldn't—"

He handed me a fag from his half-empty box. "You run out?"

"Er, yeah."

"I know how you feel. It always hits you in the middle of the bloody night, doesn't it? Got a light?"

I shook my head.

"No problem." He lit the cigarette, passed it to me and moved over for me to take a seat next to him.

I was in no mood for whiling the night away, deep in conversation about something low down on my list of priorities, so I thanked him and made my way back upstairs. He wasn't impressed.

I took one puff and started coughing my guts up. This was only to be expected though, since I hadn't tried it before. So I ignored my discomfort and continued, determined to finish the cigarette before it killed me. With the cigarette having shrunk to roughly half its original size, I coughed so much that all the smoke blew back in my face. It got up my nose, my mouth, my eyes and my hair. I stubbed out the cigarette and went back to bed. By the time morning came around, my eyes were red raw. I'd cried so much that my pillow squelched.

I looked into the light that was shining through the curtains and felt the urge to be closer to God. I prayed for him to help me. "God, just help me. Help me to sort this thing out." As I had no one apart from the kids, he was the only one I could turn to. I knew he wouldn't let me down.

I don't know whether it was divine intervention or not, but at that moment I decided to look for a B&B that might take us in for a few days. So I got out of bed and started searching.

There were lots of B&Bs in the vicinity that were only too happy to help me out when I first called. Then, when

I explained my situation, their tone changed and they referred me to someone else. At about 10 am I made a drink and spent some time with the kids. You might say that this wasn't a constructive use of time given my predicament, but it did give me a break. It stopped me from feeling depressed, or worse still, from going begging for another cigarette. I just felt so bad because they knew something was wrong but I couldn't tell them anything. So I had to let them go on thinking I was in a bad mood with them.

Half an hour later, just as I was washing my cup, my phone informed me I had received an email. I didn't think anything of it. When you're not expecting something, it usually turns out to be junk or from someone pestering you to buy something you don't want. So I left it until the cup was back in the cupboard and the kids were quiet. Then, just to satisfy my curiosity, I had a look. And wouldn't you know it, it was from Hammersmith & Fulham Social Services. They said if I was still looking for somewhere to live, they might be able to help.

This was good news that cheered me up no end, but inside I couldn't help feeling sceptical. They didn't say what kind of help they were offering. Nevertheless, I went there first thing the next morning, which was a Tuesday.

I wasn't expecting much, but whatever hopes I had were dashed once I saw the woman's smug grin. I could tell she thought I was expecting something permanent and took great delight in disappointing me.

They'd changed their tune. They were now saying that if I still needed help, they could help me, but they had some questions first. They asked if I had any local connections, so I told them about my sister. I got on the phone to her there and then, feeling hopeful that my situation would soon be resolved. I asked her for her details, which they needed so my case could be transferred. Much to my surprise and horror, she said no. I asked her to get her husband's opinion, but he said no as well.

I didn't know where to look.

She read a cross-referenced page from a book about two inches thick and rested her finger halfway along a row about a third of the way down. "You've been allocated some temporary accommodation at a hotel for two nights." It was something at least.

If I'd been expecting The Ritz, I'd have been disappointed. We managed to make the most of it though. The two days flew by without any dramas, and I soon found myself back at Hammersmith & Fulham Centre for the Homeless, cap in hand.

They gave me more temporary accommodation, this time for just one night. This hotel was in Harrow, which meant a tube ride and a long walk in the rain, which had already soaked us to the skin.

It has to be said that my first glimpse of the hotel didn't fill me with confidence. I could see a distinct lack of activity through the dirty windows, but I didn't want to dwell on it. Stood at the door, I looked down at my kids' drenched clothes and assured them that we'd soon warm up, and once the rain had died down, we'd go out and get something nice to eat.

I rang the bell. No reply. I rang again. Still nothing. I rang again, and when there was still no sound of life, I started to panic. I left it a minute and rang one more time before sitting down on the doorstep to give it a moment's thought. I had a cousin in White City who might help us.

We spent the night at my cousin's, but it felt a bit awkward, so I told her I'd be out of the way the next morning.

We arrived at the homeless office at 9.30 am and made a dash to grab the remaining free seats. When my turn finally came around, the woman took my details and said all the allocations would be given by the end of the day and to come back later.

So we went for a bite to eat at MacDonald's, looked around some shops and went back at 12.30 pm, full of renewed hope and enthusiasm. The woman remained expressionless and shook her head. She said to come back at the end of the day and try then. I thought I'd kill some time by going into a separate waiting area for a while. Once seated, however, I started thinking, trying to conjure up a solution. I started crying. A woman from the back office saw me on the CCTV and came into the waiting room to try to console me.

"I'm so sorry about this. Something will turn up soon, you'll see." She smiled at me and told me to stop crying.

It wasn't long after that that I was called through. The woman waited for me to take a seat before smiling and telling me they had something that might be suitable.

Granted, it was just one room with a separate kitchen, but we'd put up with worse. So we made ourselves comfortable and got settled in. We stayed in this flat for the next eight months.

For a while, life went by without any dramas, and gradually we started to leave our troubles behind us. But inside, something was wrong.

I started spending time on my own, staring through the window, mulling things over. It got to the stage where I couldn't bring myself to do simple chores like ironing or cleaning the kitchen. Something had to be done, or else my kids would start to suffer.

They hadn't forgotten about me at the hospital. They pulled up my records and started reeling off everything I'd had before I went to Nigeria. I told him my high blood pressure had come back and I couldn't motivate myself to do everyday chores.

He said to stay away from anything stressful and to try to stop worrying. I told him I'd try, but I couldn't give any guarantees.

The following week I left the consulting room and headed straight for the hospital pharmacy, where I exchanged a prescription for another course of antidepressants.

Chapter Fifteen
Found My Tribe

First Lockdown (February 2020)

Then Covid happened.

"Wait there!"

The kids stood screaming at the doorway.

Coughing and spluttering, my eyes watering, I ran around the flat, trying to see through the thick cloud of black smoke until I noticed it seeping through the ceiling. There was nothing I could do other than pray that the fire brigade would arrive in time. I sat by the door with the kids, holding my breath to listen for the siren and the onrushing engine noise.

Two days later, I read in the newspaper that it was an arson attack. Someone had a grudge against the guy in the flat above.

In a way, knowing that it was a planned attack against my neighbour and not some kind of defect with the building came as a relief. Then the thought struck me: if I go rocking the boat, the authorities might boot me out of the flat for someone less problematic.

I soon found myself sat alone in the front room, swiping my phone, wondering if I looked as despairing as I felt. My spirits did pick up when the kids came in from school, but things got worse the minute they went to bed. In the morning I'd get up, look in the mirror and shake my head. It was like my antidepressants were my best friends.

I had stopped watching the news, as it definitely wasn't helping my mental health. I was even beginning to believe some conspiracy theories I found on YouTube, so I stopped watching them altogether.

July 2020

Eventually they found a two-bedroom flat for us on the White City Estate, near my cousin. We'd always got on well, so it was good to feel like I had someone for once. Better still, it was unlikely I'd come home to find her in bed with Femi.

I occupied my time by searching the Internet, looking for furniture that was decent yet affordable. I bought lots of second-hand stuff. Admittedly, it wasn't what I'd envisaged for myself back in 2015, when I first met him, but it was something.

Homeschooling was fun. I thoroughly enjoyed teaching my children and I learnt so much about their interests during the Covid lockdowns. Funmi is such an explorer and would like to travel the world, while Tomi is a puzzle genius.

Tomi had started cycling, so we spent our afternoons at Ravenscourt Park, and they saw some of their friends there, social distancing or not; children didn't really understand, at least not at that age.

Once again, my kids gave me a lot of strength. I saw their happy, smiling faces that were awash with excitement, and got a huge lift. I decided that people could think what they liked, because it wasn't going to affect me or my kids. Not any more.

One of the few things I had become grateful for since Covid was being alive.

I began to appreciate the little things: the precious hugs from my children, walking in the park, the weather—miserable or not—and just life generally.

The birds sang their hearts out, children played and the smell of freshly cut grass filled the air. I put the kids in the swings and got talking to another mum, just like I had once before. On the way back I smiled at the people I passed, and they smiled back. It was like they thought I was a good person and a good mother, out with her kids on a summer's night. When people spoke into their phones, they complimented me. I couldn't work out why this was, but it elevated my mood from good to great.

I saw the woman from the park most nights while the fine weather lasted. I got to know her really well, and we swapped numbers. We became so pally that we decided to go out together. Her sister, who was watching over her kids, looked after mine too. I let my hair down, told jokes that everyone found hilarious and had a couple of glasses of wine. Everyone was amiable. I looked around and noticed that there wasn't a Nigerian face in sight.

Second Lockdown November 2020

I continued to look for second-hand furniture and ideas to decorate the flat. I also kept in touch with everyone at the church. Chris, the vicar, turned out to be a really good friend to me. So, despite the restrictions, my depression wasn't as bad as it could have been.

While forming a new life over Zoom, it wasn't the same as meeting up in person. I still made a lot of new friends though. I had some one-on-one calls with Chris, the vicar, in which we talked about everything that had gone on; but the group sessions were a lot more relaxed. We all got on well, and there were other single mums. We exchanged stories about our kids and made arrangements to go out together when restrictions were lifted.

I spent most afternoons home-schooling Tomi and Funmi, and for a break we would cycle to Ravenscourt Park and back. There wasn't really much to do other than appreciate being Covid free and enjoy my time with my children. This time reminded me to be grateful to be alive, and I made a commitment to myself to make this work and thrive.

The words of the RDM Pastor who'd said he would also have slapped his wife if he was in Femi's situation kept echoing in my head. It broke me even more, so I decided never to visit that church ever again.

I had other things to worry about, so I made an actual list of all the things I had to navigate:

- Homelessness
- Court case, as I'd heard it could take years to resolve
- Increasing my income
- Staying away from toxic people, including family
- Healing
- Getting my voice heard regardless of suppressing factors such as racism and patriarchy.

I knew I had to get to work for my own good.

Therapy

Then I hit a problem. I enjoyed being part of everything, but seeing all the happy families made me feel like a failure. Then I started to think of Femi, and a dark blanket descended.

I went to see my GP, who suggested I try therapy. I gave it some thought and decided I had nothing to lose by giving it a go, so I attended the first of six sessions. It began well, and I did get something from it, but right at the end she gave me a load of paperwork to complete, and my spirits sank. I took the forms home, attempted to make a start, but I couldn't force myself to do it. I never went back.

There was this really nice late-winter morning, midway through the second lockdown. The sun was out, making the frost on the grass sparkle, so I decided to take the kids to the local swings for an hour. When we arrived, they got playing with some other kids. I saw their mum was keeping an eye on them (from a distance), so I took the chance to have a quick look on Nextdoor. That was when I found Claire, who was offering free therapy. I messaged her right there, giving her a few details, and by the time we got back home she had replied, saying she'd be happy to take me on.

I attended my first session, more in hope than expectation, but the moment I set eyes on Claire, I knew it was going to be a completely different experience than I'd had up till now. We struck up an instant rapport, and I could feel some benefits right away.

I remember looking through the window one day and thinking how I used to get much more exercise, something I hadn't thought about for a long time. So at the first available opportunity, I went for a walk. It wasn't long before I was back on my bike, seeing the world from an entirely new perspective.

After the sixth session, I felt a shadow come over me again. My spirits lifted once I saw the kids, but I wasn't looking out of the window in the same way I had been, or getting the urge to exercise. So I looked on Nextdoor again, to see if there was anyone else. And this time I found a guy called Kelvin doing CBT. I messaged him right away and he agreed to give me twelve sessions.

For those who are not familiar with the ins and outs of CBT, it's basically a kind of talking therapy. You talk about things that are troubling you, behaviours and feelings that are unhelpful, then he computes it all. Then he further talks about the effect those behaviours and feelings have on you and others, so you can challenge and change them. It's not for everyone, but Kelvin was good at it. Kelvin also provided me with a useful list detailing how to identify healthy and unhealthy relationships, which I stuck on the wall in my bedroom.

He was so good that twelve weeks later I had come on even further than I had after Claire. One day I was walking through town and I came across this community centre with a notice outside saying they did yoga classes, so I thought, why the hell not? I have to admit that I felt vulnerable to begin with, but with all the therapists and others, I was used to this feeling by now. The classes were done via Zoom, which was handy for me on the one hand, but a bit disappointing on the other.

It didn't stop there. I started cycling every day, running, walking, going to the gym. Everything I had done before I'd met Femi. Church was every Sunday, lockdown or not. The longer it went on, the more I started to feel like I was being reacquainted with an old friend or twin. It was like he had me in a trance all this time, forcing me to walk through a dark wilderness, and now, finally, I was basking in the sun.

Chapter Sixteen
My Transformative journey

Christmas 2020

I looked around our cosy living room, decorated with twinkling lights and festive ornaments. Funmi and Tomi were playing happily with the ornaments on the Christmas tree, oblivious to the turmoil that had consumed their mother's life over the past few years.

In hindsight, I could see that the therapy had helped me heal from the trauma of all the abuse. It had also exposed that Femi wasn't the only one abusing me. My family were as well, especially my mum and my sister. Although the others hadn't been active participants, the term 'flying monkeys' came to mind, but I didn't want to tag them as such. I just had to maintain a safe distance from them all and focus on creating the life I wanted for myself and my children.

I was determined to give my children the childhood they deserved. They needed to know that they were loved and protected, and that they could achieve anything they set their minds to.

They still believed in Santa, so I gradually bought, wrapped and hid their presents in my bedroom. Got to keep the spirit of Christmas alive even though I was dreading the holidays on my own.

Christmas has always brought back a flood of memories for me. Memories of a childhood filled with love and laughter, surrounded by my family. I remember going to church with my parents and siblings. I remember my dad playing the piano in the church, and I was in the church choir singing Christmas carols. I remember coming home to a house filled with the delicious smell of my mother's fried turkey. Everything seemed to change when my dad passed away 13 years ago. Everything.

Dad was gone forever, and God did I miss him. I missed my old life and family. I missed my grandma, who'd passed away a year after my dad's demise, and I couldn't even attend her funeral. I missed home. But home wasn't the same any more. What had happened to the Alli's after Dad had died?

"Mummy, Mummy, can I have a sweetie?" Tomi tapped me on my back. "What's wrong, Mummy? You look sad."

I turned around and wiped the tears quickly. "Yes, sure. I'm not sad. It's Christmas Day. I'm happy. Are you happy, darling?"

"Yes, Mummy, I am. I love all my presents and chocolates. This is the best Christmas ever! Santa brought me all the presents, and he drank the hot chocolate too. I'm going to tell Harry when I see him that Santa came to my house." He beamed on and took another toy to his sister.

I stared at the phone in my hand, my finger hovering over the call button. I wanted to call Mum. I wanted to tell her I loved her and missed her.

But then I remembered how she had called me a disgrace. I remembered how hurt I had felt when she told me she had called my ex-dude, or whatever, to congratulate him on the birth of his son, who had been conceived just a month after I had separated from him. Why was I treated differently to my sister when she had experienced domestic abuse and needed a fresh start? I'd helped her. We all had.

A tear welled up in my eye. I loved my mother, but she had hurt me so deeply. I didn't know if I could ever forgive her.

I put the phone down and took a deep breath. There were constant reminders that I was a single mother. And it felt like the 'single' meant facing life on my own and being isolated from everyone. But I knew that although I couldn't change the past, I could control my future. I was determined to give my children the Christmas they deserved, the life they deserved, a family they could rely on.

I got up, grabbed my journal and went to the kitchen. I started preparing Christmas dinner. I made Jollof rice, turkey and fried plantain, just like I'd had when I was a little girl, and I even baked my children's favourite Christmas cookies. And while the cookies were in the oven, I scribbled down my New Year's resolutions.

Later that evening, the children and I gathered around the Christmas tree. We opened presents, sang Christmas carols and told stories. We laughed and danced to some Afrobeat songs.

May 2021

Breathing heavily, I secured my bicycle outside the school gates, my mind still grappling with disappointment from the job centre. As I approached the school, I said a rushed hello to Gloria, another Nigerian mum I'd met while doing the school run, and darted towards the first school to pick up Funmi, heart racing against the ticking clock.

After a quick hug and a promise to catch up on the day's adventures, I guided Funmi to my bike and swiftly pedalled towards the second school. The minutes seemed to tick faster than my wheels spun, but determination fuelled my every movement.

I arrived at Tomi's school just in time and strapped him into the carrier. "Mummy, can we go to the park?" he asked.

I thought about it for a second. The park wasn't such a bad idea. I replied, "Yes, we can."

As we approached Hammersmith Park, Funmi saw her friends from school and rushed to play. Tomi had a quick snack and joined them. I sat on the bench and took out my phone to catch up on emails. I looked up from time to time, and their laughter created a brief respite. As we headed home, I couldn't stop thinking about the so far unattainable course I wanted to do that held the key to my professional renaissance.

Evening settled in, and after the children were fed and tucked into bed, I opened my laptop, determined to find a solution. I scoured the Internet for alternative funding options and stumbled upon scholarships and grants tailored for women returning to the workforce. Eagerly, I filled out applications, pouring my aspirations into each form.

Days turned into weeks, and amid juggling household responsibilities, school runs and the relentless pursuit of financial aid, I received an email that warmed my heart. A local foundation had offered to cover the full cost of the business analyst course. Thank you, Lord!

Gratitude filled my heart as I updated my work coach, who shared in my joy. The restart programme's support became a guiding light as I immersed myself in the training, honing my skills into business information systems.

Week by week, the bi-weekly catchups provided reassurance, encouragement and a reminder that I was not alone on this journey. With my work coach's guidance, I polished my CV until it shone with newfound confidence.

As the course concluded, I felt a sense of accomplishment. Armed with my Master's degree and fresh skills, I set out to explore job opportunities. The support I'd received not only revitalised my career but also empowered me as a single mother, proving that a supportive community can turn the tide against adversity.

With trembling hands, I hesitated for a moment before answering the call from a withheld number. The voice on the other end delivered news that shattered the scepticisms that had settled in my heart—I had secured the business analyst position I had applied for.

Overwhelmed with emotion, I struggled to find words as the caller detailed the terms of my employment. The role was not only a match for my skills but also a blessing in terms of flexibility. In the era of COVID-19, the job was hybrid, allowing me to be in the office twice a week and work from home the remaining three days. It was the perfect arrangement that would let me balance the demands of a career with the commitments of motherhood.

As the realisation sunk in, tears of joy welled up in my eyes. The weight of years spent navigating the challenges of single parenthood suddenly lifted, replaced by the promise of stability and a sense of accomplishment. Gratitude flooded me as I thought about the countless moments of sacrifice and resilience that led to this breakthrough.

Ecstatic, I shared the news with my children, who met it with cheers and hugs. The prospect of being present for the school runs, extracurricular activities and bedtime routines while building a successful career brought a profound sense of fulfilment.

In the days that followed, I embraced my new role with enthusiasm, attending the office with a renewed sense of purpose on the designated days and seamlessly transitioning into the rhythm of working from home. The juggling act became a dance of harmony, my overall fitness was better because of the daily cycling and I marvelled at how life had unfolded, turning the page to a chapter filled with promise and opportunity.

As I wrote in my journal 'Done', I struck out 'Increase my income' and reflected on the journey that had brought me to this point. The setbacks, the resilience and the unwavering determination all converged into a narrative of triumph. And in the quiet moments of reflection, I allowed myself to shed tears, not of sorrow, but of gratitude for the resilience that had carried me to this transformative chapter in my life. And it was at that moment I decided I was going to share this story with somebody else. If I helped at least one person, it would be another box to mark 'Done'.

The year went by quickly. My birthday came, and I was finally able to treat myself to some laser hair-removal treatments and a Hydrafacial treatment I had been wanting for a while. The irony of hair growing in unwanted places and yet not on my scalp made me chuckle. Well at least I did not have to walk around with my *gorimapa* head when I could wear a wig to cover my patches (*gorimapa* in Yoruba means bald head). So I treated myself to a human-hair wig that could potentially last me another three years or so. After a decade of grappling with hair loss, I had transformed the skill of selecting wigs into an art form. Relying on them had become second nature, and now I could swiftly discern the quality of the hair, a skill that came far more effortlessly than it had years before. The Vietnamese supplier could be hearing from me in the future—I could sell them, couldn't I?

As Christmas approached, the air in our home buzzed with a different kind of excitement. The glow of holiday lights adorned the neighbourhoods and laughter echoed through the flat as we decorated the Christmas tree.

Reflecting on the past year, I marvelled at the financial independence I had gained. No longer dependent on benefits, I was able to provide for my children in ways that were once beyond my reach. The idea of taking them to Disneyland Paris had transformed from a distant dream into a tangible reality.

December arrived, and with it came Funmi's birthday, followed my Tomi's birthday in January. The usual party preparations took a different turn as I presented an envelope containing the surprise of a lifetime. The sparkle in my daughter's eyes intensified as she opened the envelope, revealing tickets to Disneyland Paris. The decision to forego traditional birthday parties in favour of this magical adventure was met with unanimous agreement from both my daughter and son.

As the day of departure neared, excitement bubbled within our family. The journey to Disneyland Paris became more than a vacation; it was a celebration of resilience, success and the magic of shared dreams. The children, wide-eyed and filled with wonder, explored the enchanting park, captivated by the whimsical characters and vibrant attractions.

For me, witnessing my children's joy mirrored the happiness I had longed to provide. As we strolled down Main Street, the nostalgic ambiance (lived through movies but with a sense of togetherness in my childhood) triggered a flood of memories from my own childhood. Disneyland, once a distant fantasy, had now become a place where I could share the enchantment of my past with the bright-eyed curiosity of my children.

The twinkling lights, the laughter and the collective thrill of the rides painted a portrait of family unity and newfound prosperity. My heart swelled with gratitude, not only for the experiences I could provide for my children, but also for the personal transformation that had brought me to this extraordinary moment.

As we bid farewell to Disneyland, I knew that this journey was not just about reaching a destination but about savouring the magical moments along the way. The echoes of laughter and the sparkle in my children's eyes were the most precious gifts of all, marking a chapter of triumph and joy in the ongoing story of my transformative journey.

Chapter Seventeen
Shattered Ties: Navigating Loss and Dysfunction in the Family Tapestry

June 2022

I was on a work call with Jane, my product owner, trying to figure out how to fix a glitch in the build of our solution. This was a genuine problem that had put us behind by at least four weeks, and we had a looming deadline from the FCA regulations. I felt a surge of panic and frustration, knowing that our reputation and credibility were at stake. But as I listened to Jane's suggestions, my phone kept buzzing from the family group chat. What now? I really didn't want to look at any more pictures of how they were playing happy families, pretending that everything was fine. They had never understood me, never supported me, never accepted me for who I was. They had made me feel like an outsider, a failure, a disappointment. And when I decided to distance myself from them, to focus on my own mental well-being, they had blamed me for breaking the family apart. I wondered if things could have been different for me and my children if they had shown me some compassion and empathy, if they had helped me through the process of unfucking myself. But no. They had only judged me, criticised me, rejected me. I felt a pang of sadness and anger, mixed with a hint of longing and regret. I quickly snapped out of it and brought myself back to the present. I took down the details of the follow-up actions Jane and I had agreed on, hoping that we could still 'save the day', but deep down, I knew I was not happy, not fulfilled, not at peace, and I felt this way every time there were messages on that damn group chat.

I was working on a report when my phone rang. It was my brother. His voice sounded shaky and urgent.

"Tinuke you need to come to the hospital right now. Mum is in a coma."

I felt a jolt of shock and disbelief. Mum had just arrived from Nigeria to the UK on holiday some weeks back. She had seemed fine, happy, healthy. What had happened to her?

"What? How? What happened?" I asked, my voice trembling.

"I don't know, Tinuke She just collapsed this morning. She had a stroke or something. They said it's serious. She might not make it."

I felt a wave of heat and nausea wash over me. My thoughts were racing and spinning. How could this be happening? Not again. Not like Dad. I remembered the phone call I had received years ago, when Dad had had a brain haemorrhage. He'd passed away a few weeks later. I remembered the pain, the grief, the guilt for been away in the UK while Dad was back home in Nigeria.

I took a deep breath and tried to calm myself. I asked him for the details of the hospital and told him I would be on my way. As I hung up the phone, I looked at my mum's WhatsApp messages from the week before. They were still unread, still unanswered. I had ignored them.

She had pleaded with me to settle with my sister. She had asked me to think of the children, to think of the family. She had begged me to forgive and forget. She had said that she was going back to Nigeria soon and that she didn't know if we would ever see each other again. She had asked me to think of that, to think of whether it made sense or not. She had waited for my reply, but I had given her none. I had been too proud, too stubborn, too hurt.

The last message she had sent me was a simple apology. She had said she was sorry for whatever 'she and her family had done to me', and that she hoped I would forgive them. I had replied with a cold and curt 'OK, thanks.' That was it. That was the last thing I had said to her.

I felt a surge of regret and remorse. I wished I had said something else, something more. I wished I had told her I loved her, I missed her, I was sorry that things had become this way. I wished I had given her a chance, a hug, a smile. I wished I had never had to experience my family break in the way it had following the separation from Femi. I wished things were different.

I grabbed my coat and keys and ran out of the door. I hoped it was not too late. I hoped I could still see her, still talk to her, still make things right. I hoped she would wake up and we could start over. I hoped she would forgive me. I hoped I could forgive myself.

I arrived at the hospital feeling nervous and anxious. I hadn't seen my siblings in ages, and I didn't know how they would react to me. I walked into the waiting room, where they were all gathered. They looked up at me with a mix of surprise, relief and resentment. I muffled some hellos and asked, "Where is Mum?"

My sister came up to me and offered me a hug. She was crying and said, "I'm sorry, Tinuke. I'm really sorry for everything I've done. Please forgive me."

I hugged her back, feeling a rush of emotions. She was the one who had started the feud, the one who had betrayed me, the one who had hurt me the most. But she was also my sister and my best friend. I had missed her, despite everything.

I asked again, "Where's Mum?"

She wiped her tears and said, "She's in the ICU. They said she's stable, but they don't know if she'll wake up. They said we can see her. You can go in when you are ready."

I nodded, feeling a lump in my throat. I looked at my other brothers, who were sitting on the chairs, looking grim. They nodded back with a hint of warmth. They had been angry with me too, but they had also tried to reach out to me, to mend the rift. They had been more understanding, more forgiving, more supportive. I felt a pang of guilt for ignoring them, for shutting them out, for hurting them too.

I followed my sister to the ICU, where a nurse was waiting. She checked my ID and said, "You're Tinuke Alli right? You're the last sibling?"

I said, "Yes, I am. Can I see her?"

She said, "Yes, you can. But only for a few minutes. And please be gentle. She's very fragile."

She led me to a room, where Mum was lying on a bed, hooked to various machines and tubes. She looked pale and thin, her eyes closed, her chest rising and falling slowly. She looked nothing like the vibrant, lively woman I had known, the woman who had raised me, the woman who had loved me.

I walked up to her bed, feeling tears welling up in my eyes. I took her hand, which was cold and limp. I said, "Mum, it's me, Tinuke. I'm here. I'm sorry. I love you."

After my mum had undergone surgery to drain some fluid from her brain, she had suffered complications that had led to her brain stem being damaged. The brain stem is the part of the brain that controls the vital functions of the body, such as breathing, heartbeat and blood pressure. Without it, there is no life.

The next three days were the most gruesome and painful days of my life. I felt like I was in a trance, numb and detached from reality. My siblings and I were called into a meeting room with the consultant and the nurse to discuss the next steps. They told us there was nothing more they could do for Mum, that she was brain dead, that she was only alive because of the machines. They told us we had to make a decision—whether to keep her on life support or let her go.

As the consultant explained the details, starting from my mum being brought in to A&E by my brother following a seizure, to the current state of her brain stem being irreversibly damaged, I felt a surge of anger and disbelief. How could this happen? How could a simple surgery go so wrong? How could they fail to save her? How could they give up on her?

He further explained that we could use the next few days while she was still on the life support machine to inform our extended family members and to say our final goodbyes. And that word triggered me. Final. That meant it was over. That meant there was no hope. That meant we had to accept the inevitable. That meant we had to lose her.

I sobbed uncontrollably, and so did my siblings. We hugged each other, trying to comfort each other, trying to find some strength in each other. We were all devastated, shattered, broken. We had lost our dad, and now we were losing our mum. We had lost our parents, and now we were losing our home. We had lost our past, and now we were losing our future.

We decided to keep Mum on life support for a few more days, hoping for a miracle, hoping for a change, hoping for a sign. We visited her every day, talking to her, praying for her, holding her hand. We told her how much we loved her, how much we missed her, how much we needed her. We told her how sorry we were, how grateful we were, how proud we were. We told her everything we wanted to say, everything we needed to say, everything we should have said.

But she never responded, never moved, never opened her eyes. She was gone, and we knew it. We had to let her go, and we knew it. We had to say goodbye, and we knew it. But we didn't want to, and we hated it.

The loss of my mum was the most devastating and heartbreaking thing that has ever happened to me. I felt like a part of me died with her, like a part of me was missing, like a part of me was empty. I felt lost, alone, hopeless. I felt angry, bitter, resentful. I felt guilty, ashamed, regretful. I felt everything and nothing at the same time.

The following year revealed a lot of depth into the dynamics of my family, insight into my own health and some lifelong lessons and guidance on how to survive the rest of my life. My mum's siblings were informed of her condition, and they turned up at intervals to the hospital. There were six of them in total, but only three of them lived in the UK. The other three lived in Nigeria, along with my grandma, who had turned 100 a year before. One of my aunties, who we hadn't seen for decades, turned up and was distraught about the death of her sister, even though they hadn't spoken for years. I often wondered why no one talked to her any more. I vividly remembered using her make-up when I was about eight years old. I remembered her being close to my mum then, but no one knew what happened. My mum always told me as a child that family was everything and I didn't need friends, and that my siblings were enough.

The next few weeks were spent planning the funeral, agreeing on a location, number of guests, etc. And even though the years that led up to this were tumultuous as siblings, surprisingly, my mum's funeral went well. We were able to put any differences aside and organise my mum's exit from earth. We had a lot of support, both financially and emotionally, from our extended family too—my cousins, my aunties, and also my dad's stepbrothers in Nigeria. The only person that was shielded from this information was my 100-year-old grandma, because according to our Yoruba tradition, if a child dies before the parent, the parent shouldn't be present at the funeral. And in this very instance, I agreed that it would have done my grandma more harm than good to learn of the loss of her daughter, who was also her main carer in Nigeria.

The funeral was a beautiful, solemn ceremony, with a lot of tears, prayers and memories. We buried my mum in a cemetery near her first home, in Camberwell, where she lived with my dad. We said our final goodbyes and thanked her for everything she had done for us, everything she had taught us, everything she had given us. We promised to honour her legacy, to live up to her expectations, to make her proud. We promised to love each other, to support each other, to stay together. We promised to never forget her, never let her go, never say goodbye.

During the months following the funeral, I started to notice some changes in my health. I started to have more inflammation on my scalp. It was very tender and sore. I had more hair loss too.

I went back to see a dermatologist, who confirmed that my condition had worsened and that I needed to reduce my stress. He told me that my condition was not curable, but manageable, and that I had to take care of myself, or else I would risk more damage to my body. My understanding of what he told me was that my condition was partly genetic, partly environmental and partly emotional, and that I had to address all these factors and manage my stress. I began to see my condition as wake-up call, a challenge, an opportunity, and I had to embrace it, not fight it, or else I would not grow.

I listened to him, and I started to make some changes in my life. I continued to take my medication, which helped me control my symptoms and prevent further harm. I made changes to my diet, which helped me nourish my body and boost my immunity. I reduced my stress, which helped me calm my mind and balance my emotions. I started to take care of myself, which helped me heal my body, my mind and my soul.

I learnt that life is precious, and that I should not take it for granted. I learnt that life is unpredictable, and that I should not expect it to be fair. I learnt that life is short, and that I should not waste it on things that don't matter. I learnt that life is a gift, and that I should be grateful for it.

Milton Keynes UK
Ingram Content Group UK Ltd.
UKHW041029260124
436746UK00004B/116

9 781803 816029